Israel Cook Russell

An Expedition to Mount St. Elias, Alaska

Israel Cook Russell

An Expedition to Mount St. Elias, Alaska

ISBN/EAN: 9783337329877

Printed in Europe, USA, Canada, Australia, Japan

Cover: Foto ©Andreas Hilbeck / pixelio.de

More available books at **www.hansebooks.com**

VOL. III, PP. 53-204, PLS. 2-20   MAY 29, 1891

THE

NATIONAL GEOGRAPHIC MAGAZINE

--- ---   ‒‒ ‒‒   ‒‒ ‒‒ ‒‒

AN EXPEDITION TO MOUNT ST. ELIAS, ALASKA

BY ISRAEL C. RUSSELL.

(*Accepted for publication March 18, 1891.*)

‒‒   ‒‒

CONTENTS.

ILLUSTRATIONS.

INTRODUCTION.

THE SOUTHERN COAST OF ALASKA.

The southern coast of Alaska is remarkable for the regularity of its general outline. If a circle a thousand miles in diameter be inscribed on a map of the northern Pacific with a point in about latitude 54° and longitude 145° as a center, a large part of its northern periphery will be found to coincide with the southern shore of Alaska between Dixon entrance on the east and the Alaska peninsula on the west. On the northern part of this great coast-circle lies the region explored in the summer of 1890 and described in the following pages.

From Cross sound, at the northern end of the great system of islands forming southeastern Alaska, westward along the base of the Fairweather range, the mountains are exceedingly rugged, and present some of the finest coast scenery in the world. There are but two inlets east of Yakutat bay on this shore which afford shelter even for small boats. These are Lituya bay and Dry bay. Ships may enter Lituya bay, at certain stages of the tide; and find a safe harbor within; but the approaches to Dry bay are not navigable. West of Yakutat bay the coast is equally inhospitable all the way to Prince William sound.

As if to compensate for the lack of refuge on either end, there is in the center of this great stretch of rock-bound coast, over 300 miles in extent, a magnificent inlet known as Yakutat bay, in which a thousand ships could find safe anchorage. On some old maps this bay is designated as " Baie de Monti," "Admiralty bay " and " Bering bay," as will be seen when its discovery and history are discussed on another page.

The southern shore of Alaska, for a distance of 200 miles along the bases of the Fairweather and St. Elias ranges, is formed of a low table-land intervening between the mountains and the sea. Yakutat bay is the only bight in this plateau sufficiently deep to reach the mountain to the northward. This bay has a broad opening to the sea ; the distance between its ocean capes is twenty miles, and its extension inland is about the same. Its eastern shore is fringed with low, wooded islands, among which are sheltered harbors, safe from every wind that blows. The most accessible of these is Port Mulgrave, near its entrance on the eastern side.

The shores of Yakutat bay, on both the east and the west, are low and densely wooded for a distance of twenty-five miles from the ocean, where the foot-hills of the mountains begin. ' At the head of the bay the land rises in steep bluffs and forms pictur- esque mountains, snow-capped the year round. These high- lands, although truly mountainous in their proportions, are but the foot-hills of still nobler uplifts immediately northward. The bay extends through an opening in the first range to the base of the white peaks beyond. This opening was examined a century ago by explorers in search of the delusive " Northwest passage," in the hope that it would lead to the long-sought "Strait of Annan "—the dream of many voyagers. It was surveyed by the expedition in command of Malaspina in 1792, and on account of his frustrated hopes was named " Puerto del Desengaño," or " Disenchantment bay," as it has been rendered by English writers.

The waters of Yakutat and Disenchantment bays are deep, and broken only by islands and reefs along their eastern shores. A few soundings made in Disenchantment bay within half a mile of the land showed a depth of from 40 to 120 fathoms. The swell of the ocean is felt up to the very head of the inlet, indi- cating, as was remarked to me by Captain C. L. Hooper, that there are no bars or reefs to break the force of the incoming swells.

The lowlands bordering Yakutat bay on the southeast are composed of assorted glacial débris. Much of the country is low and swampy, and is reported to contain numerous lakelets. Northwest of the bay the plateau is higher than toward the southeast, and has a general elevation of about 500 feet at a distance of a mile from the shore; but the height increases toward the interior, where a general elevation of 1,500 feet is attained over large areas. All of this plateau, excepting a narrow fringe along the shore, is formed by a great glacier, belonging to what is termed in this paper the *Piedmont* type. There are many reasons for believing that the plateau southeast of Yakutat bay was at one time covered by a glacier similar to the one now existing on the northwest.*

The mountains on the northern border of the seaward-stretching table-lands, both southeast and northwest of Yakutat bay, are abrupt and present steep southward-facing bluffs. This escarpment is formed of stratified sandstones and shales, and owes its origin to the upheaval of the rocks along a line of fracture. In other words, it is a gigantic fault scarp. The gravel and bowlders forming the plateau extending oceanward have been accumulating on a depressed orographic block (or mass of strata moved as a unit by mountain-making forces), which has undergone some movement in very recent times, as is recorded by a terrace on the fault scarp bordering it. West of Yakutat the geological structure is more complex, and long mountain spurs project into the platform of ice skirting the ocean. Filling the valleys between the mountain spurs, there are many large seaward-flowing glaciers, tributary to the great Piedmont ice-sheet.

This brief sketch of the geography of Yakutat bay, together with the accompanying outline map of Alaska (plate 2), will, it is hoped, aid in making intelligible the following historical sketch and the narrative of the present expedition.

* This matter will be discussed in part IV of this paper, where it is also shown that Yakutat bay itself was formerly occupied by glacial ice.

PART I

PREVIOUS EXPLORATIONS IN THE ST. ELIAS REGION.*

BERING, 1741.

The first discovery of the southern coast of Alaska was made by Vitus Bering and Alexei Cherikof, in the vessels *St. Peter* and *St. Paul*, in 1741. On July 20 of that year, Bering saw the mountains of the mainland, but anchored his vessels at Kyak island, 180 miles west of Yakutat bay, without touching the continental shore. A towering, snow-clad summit northeast of Kyak island was named " Mount St. Elias," after the patron saint of the day.

COOK, 1778.

The next explorer to visit this portion of Alaska was Captain James Cook, who sailed past the entrance of Yakutat bay on May 4, 1778. Thinking that this was the bay in which Bering anchored, he named it " Bering's bay." Mount St. Elias was seen in the northwest at a distance of 40 leagues, but no attempt was made to measure its height.

LA PÉROUSE, 1786.†

Yakutat bay, in which we are specially interested, was next seen by the celebrated French navigator, J. F. G. de la Pérouse, in command of the frigates *La Boussole* and *L'Astrolabe*, on June 23, 1786.

The chart showing the route followed by La Pérouse during this portion of his voyage is reproduced in plate 3. In the splendid atlas accompanying the narrative of his travels, the explorer pictures the quaint, high-pooped vessels in which he cir-

---

* For more complete bibliographic references than space will allow in this paper, the reader is referred to Dall and Baker's " Partial list of books, pamphlets, papers in serials, journals and other publications on Alaska and adjacent regions;" in Pacific Coast Pilot : Coasts and Inlets of Alaska ; second series. U. S. Coast and Geodetic Survey, Washington, 1879; 4°, pp. 225-375.

† Voyage de la Pérouse autour du monde. Four vols., 1°, and atlas; Paris, 1797 ; vol. 2, pp. 130-150.

cumnavigated the globe. These French frigates were the first to cruise off Yakutat bay. The last vessel to navigate those waters was the United States revenue steamer *Corwin*, which took our little exploring party on board in September, 1890, and then steamed northward to the ice-cliffs at the head of Disenchantment bay. So far as I am aware, the *Corwin* is the only vessel that has floated on the waters of that inlet north of Haenke island. One hundred years has made a revolution in naval architecture, but has left this portion of the Alaska coast still unexplored.

La Pérouse sailed northward from the Sandwich islands, and first saw land, which proved to be a portion of the St. Elias range, on June 23. At first the shore was obscured by fog, which, as stated in the narrative of the voyage, "suddenly disappearing, all at once disclosed to us a long chain of mountains covered with snow, which, if the weather had been clear, we would have been able to have seen thirty leagues farther off. We discovered Bering's Mount Saint Elias, the summit of which appeared above the clouds."

The first view of the land is described as not awakening the feelings of joy which usually accompany the first view of an unknown shore after a long voyage. To quote the navigator's own words:

"Those immense heaps of snow, which covered a barren land without trees, were far from agreeable to our view. The mountains appeared a little remote from the sea, which broke against a bold and level land, elevated about a hundred and fifty or two hundred fathoms. This black rock, which appeared as if calcined by fire, destitute of all verdure, formed a striking contrast to the whiteness of the snow, which was perceptible through the clouds; it served as the base to a long ridge of mountains, which appeared to stretch fifteen leagues from east to west. At first we thought ourselves very near it, the summit of the mountains appeared to be just over our heads, and the snow cast forth a brightness calculated to deceive eyes not accustomed to it; but in proportion as we advanced we perceived in front of the high ground hillocks covered with trees, which we took for islands."

After some delay, on account of foggy weather, an officer was despatched to the newly discovered land; but on returning he reported that there was no suitable anchorage to be found. It is difficult at this time to understand the reason for this adverse report, unless a landing was attempted on the western side of Yakutat bay, where there are no harbors.

The name "Baie de Monti" was given to the inlet in honor of De Monti, the officer who first landed. The location of this bay, as described in the narrative and indicated on the map accompanying the report of the voyage, shows that it corresponds with the Yakutat bay of modern maps.

Observations made at this time by M. Dagelet, the astronomer of the expedition, determined the elevation of Mount St. Elias to be 1,980 toises. Considering the toise as equivalent to 6.39459 English feet, this measurement places the elevation of the mountain at 12,660 feet. What method was used in making this measurement is not recorded, and we have therefore no means of deciding the degree of confidence to be placed in it.

After failing to find an anchorage at Yakutat bay, La Pérouse sailed eastward, and on June 29 discovered another bay, which he supposed to be the inlet named "Bering's bay" by Captain Cook. It will be remembered that Cook's "Bering's bay" is Yakutat bay as now known. It is evident that the French navigator made an error in his identification, as the inlet designated as Bering's bay on his chart corresponds with that now known as Dry bay. On the maps referred to, a stream is represented as emptying into the head of this bay and rising a long distance northward; this is evidently Alsek river, the existence of which was for a long time doubted, but has recently been established beyond all question.

Finding it impossible to enter Dry bay, La Pérouse continued eastward and discovered Lituya bay, as now known, but which he named "Port des Francais." Here his ships anchored, after experiencing great difficulty in entering the harbor, and remained for many days, during which trade was carried on with the Indians, while surveys were made of the adjacent shores.

Dixon, 1787.*

Although the actual discovery of Yakutat bay is to be credited to the French, the first exploration of its shores was made by an English captain. On May 23, 1787, Captain George Dixon anchored his vessel, the *Queen Charlotte*, within the shelter of its southeastern cape, and, in honor of Constance John Phipps, Lord Mulgrave, named the haven there discovered "Port Mul-

* The Voyage around the World; but more particularly to the Northwest Coast of America. Performed in 1788-1789, in the *King George* and *Queen Charlotte*; Captains Portlock and Dixon: 4°. London, 1789.

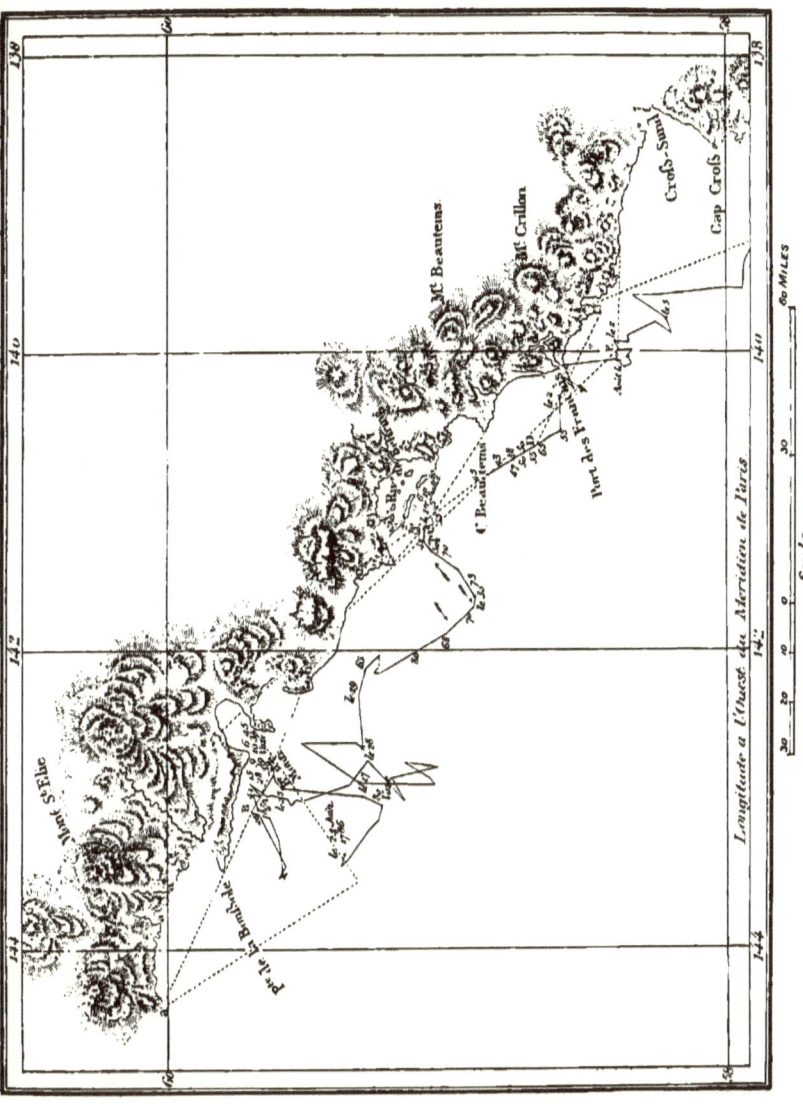

MAP OF THE ST. ELIAS REGION, AFTER LA PÉROUSE.

grave." The harbor is described in the narrative of Dixon's voyage as being "entirely surrounded by low, flat islands, where scarcely any snow could be seen, and well sheltered from any winds whatever."

The voyage of the *Queen Charlotte* was not made for the purpose of increasing geographic knowledge, but with a commercial object. Trade was at once opened with the natives, but resulted less favorably than was desired, as only sixteen sea-otter skins and a few less valuable furs were secured.

On the chart accompanying the narrative of Dixon's voyage the inlet now known as Yakutat bay is named "Admiralty bay."

A survey of the adjacent shores and inlets was made, and the astronomical position of the anchorage was approximately determined. The map resulting from these surveys, the first ever made of any portion of Yakutat bay, is reproduced on a reduced scale as plate 4.

At the time of Dixon's voyage, the inhabitants numbered about seventy, including men, women, and children, and were thus described:

"They are of about middle size, their limbs straight and well shaped, but, like the rest of the inhabitants we have seen on the coast, are particularly fond of painting their faces with a variety of colors, so that it is not any easy matter to discover their real complexion."

An amusing instance is narrated of inducing a woman to wash her face, when it was discovered that—

"Her countenance had all the cheerful glow of an English milk maid, and the healthy red which flushed her cheeks was even *beautifully* contrasted with the whiteness of her neck; her eyes were black and sparkling; her eyebrows the same color, and most beautifully arched; her forehead so remarkably clear that the transparent veins were seen meandering even in their minutest branches—in short, she was what would be reckoned as handsome even in England. The symmetry of her features, however, was marred, at least in the eyes of her English admirer, by the habit of wearing a labret in the slit of her lower lip."

During our recent visit to Port Mulgrave we did not find the native women answering to the glowing description of the voyager who discovered the harbor; but this may be owing to the fact that we did not prevail upon any of them to wash their faces.

One other discrepancy must be noted between the records of Dixon's voyage and my own observations, made one hundred years later. The houses of the natives are described in the narrative just cited as—

"The most wretched hovels that can possibly be conceived: a few poles stuck in the ground, without order or regularity, recrossed and covered with loose boards. * * * quite insufficient to keep out the snow and rain."

While this description would apply to the temporary shelters now used by the Yakutat Indians when on their summer hunting and fishing expeditions, it by no means describes the houses in which they pass the winter. These are large and substantially built of planks hewn from spruce trees, and in some instances supported from the inside by four huge posts, carved and painted to represent grotesque figures. In the center of the roof there is a large opening through which the smoke escapes from the fire kindled in an open space in the floor. But few of the Indian villages of Alaska, excepting perhaps the homes of the Thlinkets in the Alexandrian archipelago, are better built or more comfortable than those at Port Mulgrave.

On the map of Port Mulgrave already referred to, " Point Turner " and " Point Carrew " appear. The former was named for the second mate of the *Queen Charlotte*, who was the first of her officers to land ; the second name was probably designed to honor another officer of the expedition, but of this I am not positive.

DOUGLAS, 1788.*

In 1788, another trading vessel, the ship *Iphigenia*, in command of Captain Douglas, visited the southern shore of Alaska and anchored in Yakutat bay ; but no special account of the country or the inhabitants is recorded in the narrative of the voyage.

MALASPINA, 1792.†

About a hundred years ago the interest felt by the maritime nations of Europe in a " Northwest passage," connecting the

* Voyage of the *Iphigenia* ; Captain Douglas : in Voyages made in the years 1788–1789 from China to the Northwest Coast of America. John Meares, 4°, London, 1790.

† Relacion del viage hecho por las goletas Sutil y Mexicana en el año de 1792 para reconocer el estrecho de Fuca ; con una introduccion en que se da noticia de las expediciones executadas anteriormente por los Españoles en busca del paso del noroeste de la América [Por Don Dionisio Alcala Galiano]. Madrid, 1802 [accompanied by an atlas]. Pp. CXII–CXXI.

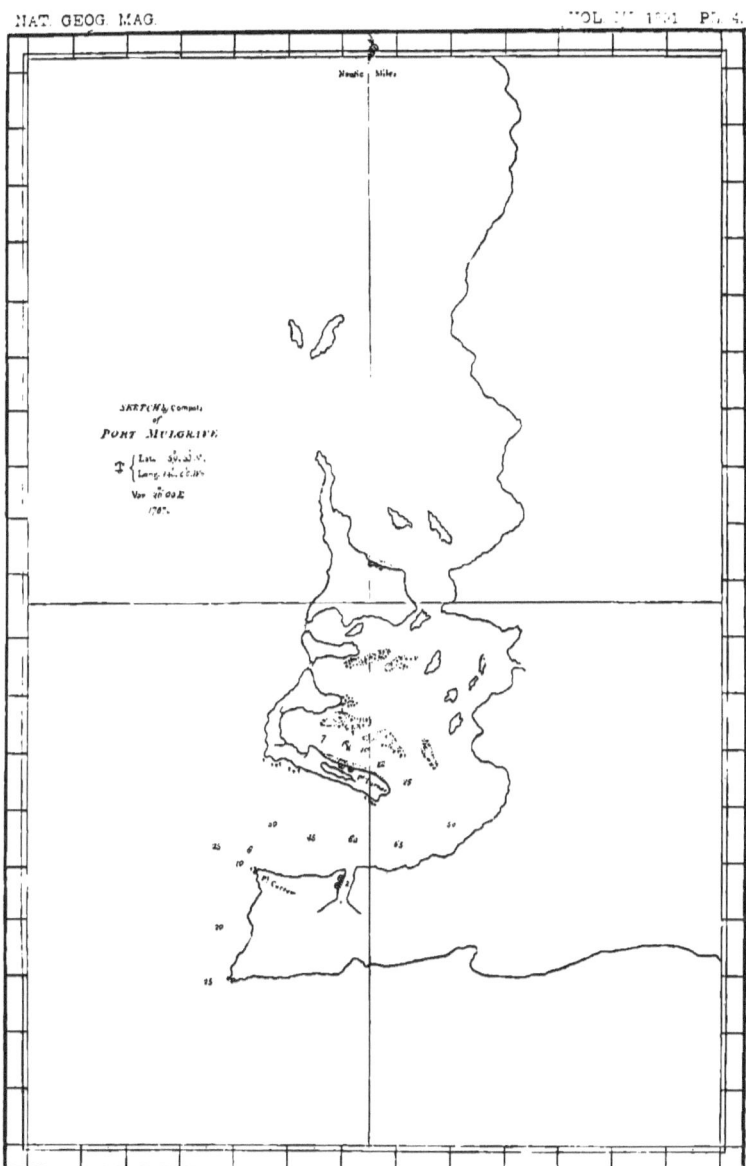

MAP OF THE EASTERN SHORE OF YAKUTAT BAY, AFTER DIXON.

northern Atlantic with the northern Pacific, was revived by the renewal of the discussion as to the authenticity of Maldonado's reported discovery of the "Strait of Annan." The western entrance to this strait was supposed to be about in the position of Yakutat bay. Spain, in particular, after three hundred years of exploration and discovery in all parts of the world, was still anxious to extend her conquests, and, if possible, to discover the long-sought "Northwest passage." Two of her ships, the *Descubierta* and *Atrevida*, were then at Acapulco, in command of Don Alejandro Malaspina, who was engaged in a voyage of discovery.

Malaspina, like Columbus, was a native of Italy in the service of Spain. Orders were sent to him to cruise northward and test the truth of Maldonado's report. The narrative of this voyage is supposed to have been written by Don Dionisio Alcala Galiano, but his name does not appear on the title page. Still more curious is the fact that Malaspina's name is omitted from the narrative of his own voyage. On his return to Spain, he was thrown into prison, on account of court intrigues, and his discoveries were suppressed for many years.

Malaspina left Acapulco on the first of May, 1791, and reached the vicinity of the present site of Sitka on June 25. Two days later, Mount Fairweather, or "Monte Buen-tiempo," as it is designated on Spanish maps, was sighted. Continuing northwestward, the entrance to Yakutat bay was reached. The opening through the first range of mountains at its head seemed to correspond to Maldonado's description of the entrance to the mythical "Strait of Annan."

The eastern shore of Yakutat bay, called "Almiralty bay" on the Spanish chart, was explored, and an excursion was made in boats into Disenchantment bay as far as Haenke island. "Disenchantment bay," as the name appears on modern charts, was named "Desengaño bay" by Malaspina, as previously stated, in allusion to the frustration of his hopes on not finding a passage leading to the Atlantic. Explorations in Disenchantment bay were checked by ice, which descended from the north and filled all of the inlets north of Haenke island. This is indicated on the map forming plate 7 (page 68), which is reproduced from the atlas accompanying the narrative of Malaspina's voyage. Special interest attaches to this map for the reason that by comparing it with that forming plate 8 (page 75), made 100 years later, the retreat of the glaciers during that interval can be determined.* At the time of Malaspina's expedition, the Hubbard and Dalton glaciers were united, and were probably also joined by some of the neighboring glaciers which do not now reach tide-water; the whole forming a confluent ice stream which occupied all of Disenchantment bay northeast of Haenke island.

A portion of the general map of the coast of southern Alaska, showing the route followed by the *Descubierta* and the *Atrevida*, and depicting the topography of the adjacent shores, has been reproduced in plate 5. It will be noticed that on this map Lituya bay is called " Pt. des Francais," while Dry bay is designated as " Bering's bay." These and other names were adopted from the maps of La Pérouse. A map of " Bahia de Monti," from Malaspina's report, is reproduced in plate 6.

An extract from Galiano's account of Malaspina's discoveries in Yakutat and Disenchantment bays,† translated by Robert Stein, of the U. S. Geological Survey, is here inserted, in order that the reader may be able to form an independent judgment of the value of the evidence just referred to as bearing on the retreat of the glaciers:

"An observatory was established on shore, and some absolute altitudes were taken in order to furnish a basis for the reckoning of the watches; but the great concourse of Indians, their importunity and thievishness, made it necessary to transfer all the instruments on board. Still the latitude was determined, the watches were regulated, the number of oscillations made by the simple pendulum was observed, and the height of Mount St. Elias was measured, being 6,507.6 varas [17,847 feet] above sea-level. The launches being ready, put to sea on July 2 with the commander of the expedition, in order to reconnoitre the channel promised by the opening, similar to that depicted by Ferrer Maldonado in his voyage; but the small force of the tide noticed at the entrance, and the indications of the natives, made it plain not only that the desired passage did not exist there, but that the extent of the channel was very short; which was also rendered evident by the perpetual frost covering the inner west shore. The launches anchored there, having penetrated into the channel with great difficulty, the oars being clogged by the floating masses of snow; they measured a base, made some marks, gathered various objects and stones for the naturalists, and, having reached the line of perpetual frost,

* It must be remembered, however, that the map, plate 8, is not from detailed surveys; the portion referred to was sketched from a few stations only and is much generalized.

† Ibid., pp. XCIV–CXVI.

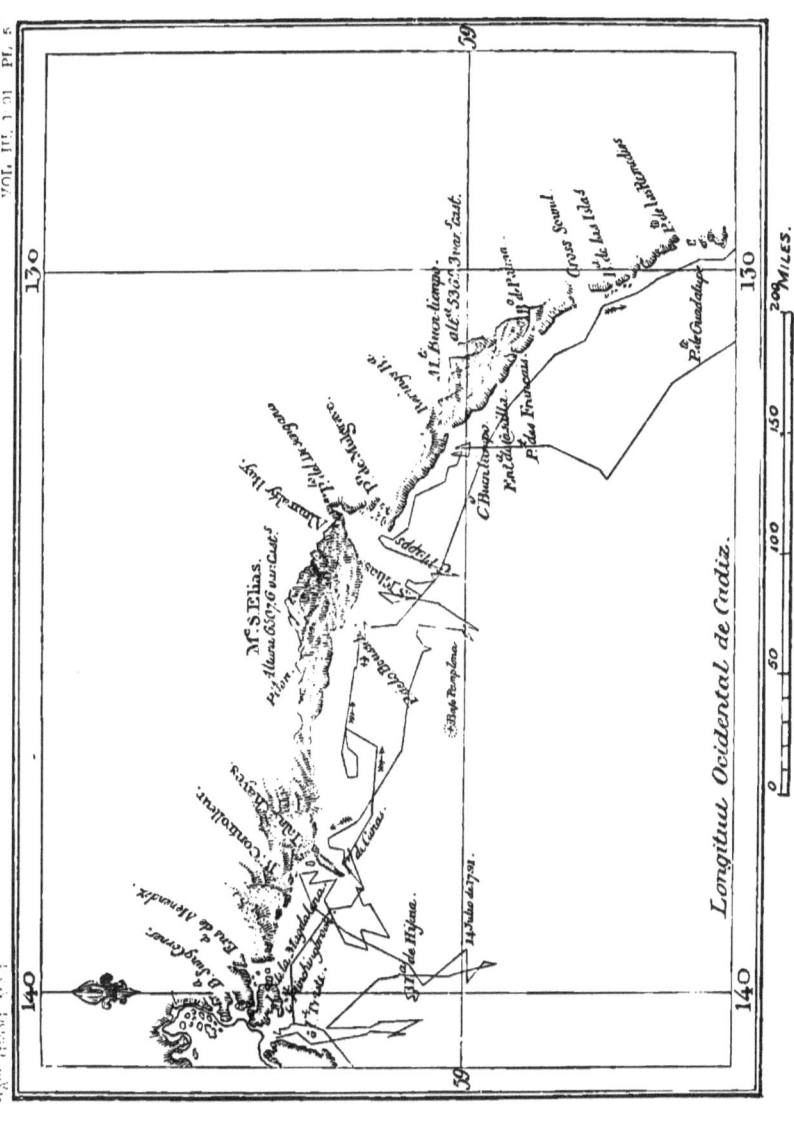

Scale.

MAP OF THE ST. ELIAS REGION, AFTER MALASPINA.

returned to the bay where they had anchored. [*] They there observed the
latitude to be 59° 59′ 30″, and six azimuths of the sun, which gave the
variation of the needle as 32° 49′. Before leaving that anchorage the commander buried a bottle with record of the reconnoissance and possession
taken in the name of the king. They called the harbor Desngaño, the
opening Bahia de las Bancas, and the island in the interior Haenke, in
memory of D. Tadeo Haenke, botanist and naturalist of the expedition.
On the third day they set out on their voyage to Mulgrave, where they
arrived on the 6th, after reconnoitering various channels and islands north
of that port and mapping them."

Following the portion of the narrative above quoted, there is
an account of the natives, containing much information of
interest to ethnologists, but which it is not necessary to follow
in a geographic report. On July 5 the corvettes sailed westward, and made a reconnoissance as far as Montegue island.
Returning eastward, they again sighted Mount St. Elias on
July 22.

"On the 28th they were three leagues west of the capes which terminate
in Bering bay [Dry bay]; the mountain of that name being about five
leagues distant from the coast and rising 5,368.3 varas [14,722 feet] above
the sea-level, and in latitude 59° 0′ 42″ and longitude 2° 4′ from Port
Mulgrave."

Mount Bering does not appear on any map that I have seen.
Which of the numerous high peaks in the vicinity of Dry bay
should be designated by that name remains to be determined.

In a record of the astronomical work of Malaspina's expedition † there are some interesting observations on the position
and elevation of Mount St. Elias, a translation of which, by Mr.
Stein, is here given :

"True longitude of Mulgrave west of Cadiz, 133° 24′ 12″. On the same
day, the 30th of June [1792], at the observatory of Mulgrave, at 6h. 30′ in
the morning, the true altitude of the sun was observed to be 16° 14′ 20″,
and its inclination being 23° 11′ 30″ and the latitude 59° 34′ 20″, the true
azimuth of the sun from north to east was concluded to be 71° 43′ 0″.
But having measured on the same occasion with the theodolite 110° 33′
from the sun's vertical to the vertical of Mount St. Elias, the difference
between these two quantities is the astronomic azimuth. Hence, from

* On the coast of the mainland east of Knight island.—I. C. R.

† Memorias sobre las observaciones astronomicas hechas por los nave-
gantes Españoles en distintos lugares del globe; Por Don Josef Espinosa
y Tello. Madrid, en la Imprente real, Año de 1809, 2 vols., large 8°; vol.
1, pp. 57–60.

the observatory of Mulgrave, said mountain bears N. 38° 50′ W., a distance of 55.1 miles, deduced by means of good observations from the ends of a sufficient base. A quadrant was used to measure the angle of apparent altitude of the mountain, 2° 38′ 6″, and allowing for terrestrial refraction, which is one-tenth of the distance of 55.1 miles, the true altitude was found to be 2° 34′ 39″; whence its elevation above sea-level was concluded to be 2,793 toises [17,860 feet], and the length of the tangent to the horizon, 152 miles, allowance being made for the increase due to terrestrial refraction * * *.

" Lastly, with the rhumb, or astronomic azimuth, and the distance from the observatory of Mulgrave to Mount St. Elias, it was ascertained that that mountain was 43′ 15″ to the north and 1° 9′ to the west, whence its latitude is found to be 60° 17′ 35″ and its longitude 131° 33′ 10″ west of Cadiz."

Taking the longitude of Cadiz as 6° 19′ 07″ W. (San Sebastian light-house), the longitude of St. Elias from this determination would be 140° 52′ 17″ W.

VANCOUVER, 1794.*

The next vessels to visit Yakutat bay after Malaspina's voyage, so far as known, were the *Discovery* and *Chatham*, under command of Captain George Vancouver. This voyage increased knowledge of the geography of southern Alaska more than any that preceded it, and was also of greater importance than any single expedition of later date to that region. The best maps of southern Alaska published at the present day are based largely on the surveys of Vancouver.

The *Discovery*, under the immediate command of Vancouver, and the *Chatham*, in charge of Peter Puget, cruised eastward along the southern coast of Alaska in 1794. The *Discovery* passed the entrance to Yakutat bay without stopping, but the *Chatham* anchored there, and important surveys were carried on under Puget's directions.

On June 28, the *Discovery* was in the vicinity of Icy bay, where the shore of the ocean seemed to be composed of solid ice. Eastward from Icy bay the coast is described as " bordered by lowlands rising with a gradual and uniform ascent to the foot-hills of lofty mountains, whose summits are but the base from which Mount St. Elias towers magnificently into the regions of per-

---

* A Voyage of Discovery to the Northern Pacific Ocean and around the World, 1790–'95; new edition, 6 vols., London, 1801. The citations which follow are from vol. 5, pp. 348–407.

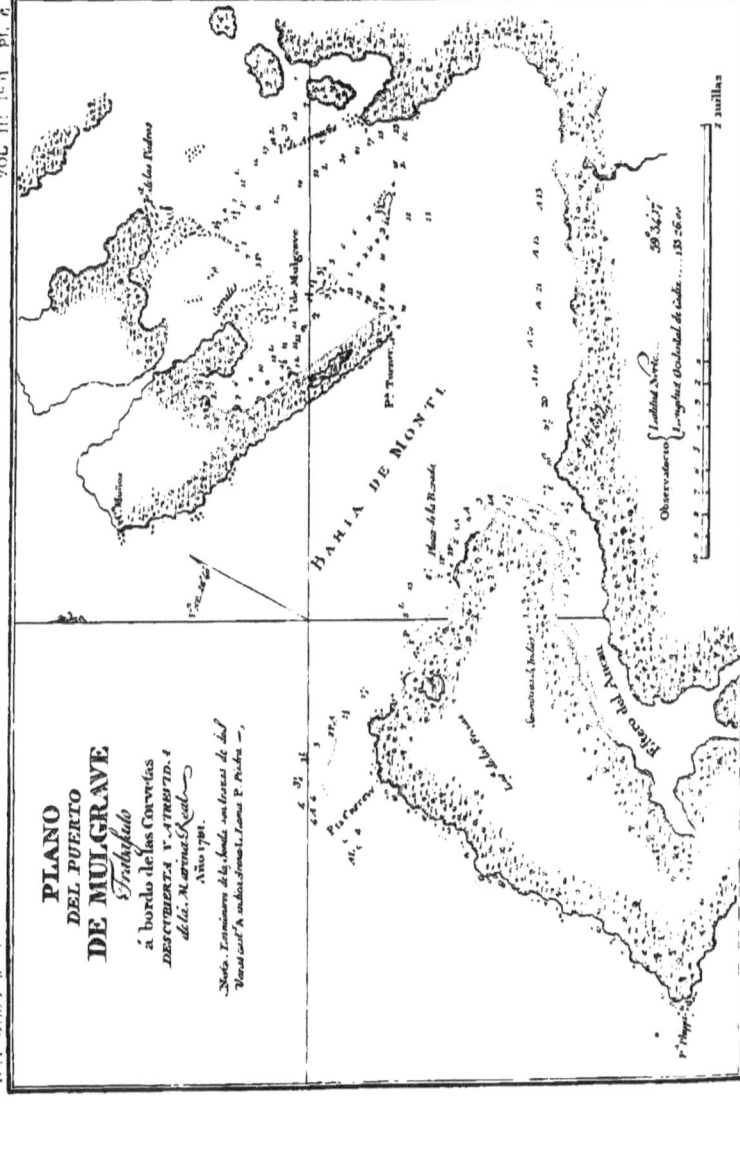

PLANO
DEL PUERTO
DE MULGRAVE
Trabajado
á bordo de las Corvetas
DESCUBIERTA Y ATREVIDA
de la Marina Real.
Año 1791.

Nota. Las sondas de la banda meridional de los
Vasos con A, ambas términos, llaman P. Pedro —,

BAHIA DE MONTI

P. Turner.

Punta de la Rivada

Pico del Puerto

Observatorio { Latitud Norte 59 34,8
{ Longitud Occidental de Cadiz . . 138 26,0

2 millas

MAP OF BAY DE MONTI AFTER MALASPINA.

petual frost." A low projecting point on the western side of the
entrance to Yakutat bay was named " Point Manby." The coast
beyond this toward the northeast became less wooded, and seemed
to produce only a brownish vegetation, which farther eastward
entirely disappeared. The country was then bare and composed
of loose stones. The narrative contains an interesting account
of the grand coast scenery from St. Elias to the eastern end of
the Fairweather range; but this does not at present claim attention.

While the *Chatham* continued her cruise eastward, Puget ascended Yakutat bay nearly to its head, and also navigated some
of the channels between the islands along its eastern shore. A
cape on the eastern side, where the bay penetrates the first range
of foot-hills, was named " Point Latouche;" but the same land-
mark had previously been designated " Pa. de la Esperanza "
by Malaspina. The bay at the head of the inlet, which Malaspina had named " Desangaño," was named " Digges sound,"
after one of the officers of the *Chatham*. Boats were sent to explore this inlet, but found it "closed from side to side by a firm,
compact body of ice, beyond which, to the back of the ice, a small
inlet appeared to extend N. 55° E. about a league." *

These observations confirm those made by Malaspina and indicated on the chart reproduced on plate 7, where the ice front
is represented as reaching as far south as Haenke island.

The evidence furnished by Malaspina and Vancouver as to
the former extent of the glaciers at the head of Yakutat bay is
in harmony with observations made by Vancouver's party in Icy
strait and Cross sound.† Early in July, 1794, these straits were
found to be heavily encumbered with floating ice. At the present time but little ice is met with in that region. On Vancouver's
charts there is no indication that he was aware of the existence
of Glacier bay, although one of his officers, in navigating Icy
strait, passed its immediate entrance. These records, although
somewhat indefinite and of negative character, indicate that the
fields of floating ice at the mouth of Glacier bay were much more
extensive a hundred years ago than at present; but they do not
show where the glaciers of that region formerly terminated.

After the return of the *Chatham's* boats from the exploration of

* Vancouver's Voyage, vol. 5, p. 389.
† Ibid., pp. 417–421.

Disenchantment bay, an exploration of the eastern shore of Yakutat bay was made. The following extract indicates the character of work done there:

"Digges' sound [Disenchantment bay] was the only place in the bay that presented the least prospect of any interior navigation, and this was necessarily very limited by the close connected range of lofty snowy mountains that stretched along the coast at no great distance from the seaside. Mr. Puget's attention was next directed to the opening in the low land, but as the wind was variable and adverse to the progress of the vessel, a boat was again despatched to continue the investigation of these shores, which are compact from Point Latouche and were then free from ice. This opening was found to be formed by an island about two miles long, in a direction S. 50° E. and N. 59° W., and about a mile broad, lying at the distance of about half a mile from the mainland. Opposite to the south part of this, named by Mr. Puget KNIGHT'S ISLAND, is Eleanor's cove, which is the eastern extremity of Beering's [Yakutat] bay, in latitude 59° 44', longitude 220° 51'. Knight's island admits of a navigable passage all round it, but there is an islet situated between it and the mainland on its northeast side. From Eleanor's cove the coast takes a direction S. 30° W. about six miles to the east point of a channel leading to the southwest, between the continent and some islands that lie off it. This was considered to lead along the shores of the mainland to Point Mulgrave, and in the event of its proving navigable, the examination of the bay would have been complete, and the vessel brought to our appointed place of meeting, which was now supposed to be no very great distance."

In endeavoring to reach Port Mulgrave by a channel leading between the islands on the eastern side of the bay and the mainland, the *Chatham* grounded, and was gotten off with considerable difficulty. Many observations concerning the geography and the natives are recorded in the narrative of this exploration.

BELCHER, 1837.[*]

The next account [†] of explorations around Yakutat bay that

* Narrative of a Voyage round the World, performed in the ship *Sulphur* during the years 1836–1842; by Captain Sir Edward Belcher: 2 vols., 8°, London, 1843.

† A fort was built by the Russians, in 1795, on the strip of land separating Bay de Monti from the ocean, and was colonized by convicts from Russia. In 1805, all of the settlers were killed and the fort was destroyed by the Yakutat Indians. So complete was this massacre that no detailed account of it has ever appeared. (Alaska and its Resources, by W. H. Dall, 1870, pp. 316, 317, 323.)

MAP OF DISENCHANTMENT BAY, AFTER MALASPINA.

has come to hand is by Sir Edward Belcher, who visited that coast in Her Majesty's ship *Sulphur* in 1837.

In the narrative of this voyage, a brief account is given of the ice cliffs at Icy bay, which are stated to have a height of about thirty feet and to present the appearance of veined marble. Where the ice was exposed to the sea it was excavated into alcoves and archways, recalling to the narrator's mind the Chalk cliffs of England. "Point Riou," as named by Vancouver, was not recognized, and the inference seems to be that it was formed of ice and was dissolved away between the visits of Vancouver and Belcher.

Accompanying the narrative of Belcher's voyage is an illustration showing Mount St. Elias as it appears from the sea near Icy bay, which represents the mountain more accurately than some similar pictures published more recently.

The *Sulphur* anchored in Port Mulgrave; but no account is given of the character of the surrounding country.

Tebenkof, 1852.[*]

Tebenkof's notes, which are often referred to by writers on Alaska, consist principally of compilations from reports of Russian traders, which were intended to accompany and explain an atlas of the shores of northwestern America, published in 1852 in St. Petersburg and in Sitka.

Map number 7 of the atlas represents the southern coast of Alaska from Lituya bay westward to Icy bay. On the same sheet there is a more detailed chart of the islands along the eastern border of Yakutat bay.

The height of St. Elias is given as 17,000 feet; its position, latitude 61° 2' 6" and longitude 140° 4', distant 30 miles from the sea.[†] It is stated that in 1839 the mountain "began at times to smoke through a crater on its southeastern slope." At the time of an earthquake at Sitka (1847) it is said to have emitted flames and ashes.

[*] Atlas of the Northwest Coast of America from Bering strait to Cape Corrientes and the Aleutian Islands [etc.]: 2°, St. Petersburg, 1852. With index and hydrographic observations: 8°, St. Petersburg, 1852.

[†] In a foot-note on page 33 it is stated that Captain Vasilef, in the ship *Okrytie* (*Discovery*), ascertained the height of Mount Fairweather to be 13,946 feet.

It will be seen from the account of the exploration carried on last summer that Mount St. Elias is composed of stratified rocks, with no indication of volcanic origin; and these reports of eruption must consequently be considered erroneous.

The low country between Mount St. Elias and the sea is described by Tebenkof as a tundra covered with forests and grass: "through cracks in the gravelly soil, ice could be seen beneath." More recent knowledge shows that this statement also is erroneous. The adjacent ocean is stated to be shallow, with shelving bottom; at a distance of half a verst, five to twelve fathoms were obtained, and at two miles from land, thirty to forty fathoms (of seven feet).

The Pimpluna rocks are said to have been discovered in 1779 by the Spanish captain Arteiga. They were also seen in 1794 by the helmsman Talin, in the ship *Orel*, and named after his vessel. These observations are interesting, and indicate that possibly there may be submerged moraines in the region where these rocks are reported to exist.

Many other observations are recorded concerning the mountains and the bays in the vicinity of Yakutat. While of interest to navigation and to geographers, these have no immediate connection with the region explored during the recent expedition.

United States Coast and Geodetic Survey, 1874,[*] 1889.[†]

The surveys carried on in 1874 by the United States Coast Survey on the shores of Alaska embraced the region about Yakutat bay. They were conducted by W. H. Dall and Marcus Baker. Besides the survey of the coast-line, determinations were made of the heights and positions of several mountain peaks between Glacier bay and Cook inlet. Dall's account of this survey contains a brief sketch of previous explorations and a summary of the measurements of the higher peaks of the region. This material has been used on another page in discussing the height of Mount St. Elias.

Besides the geographic data gathered by the United States Coast Survey, many observations were made on geology and on the glaciers of the region about Yakutat bay and Mount St. Elias. Exception must be taken, in the light of more recent

---

[*] Appendix No. 10, Report of the Superintendent of the U. S. Coast Survey for the year 1875; Washington, 1878, pp. 157–188.

[†] Pacific Coast Pilot, Alaska, part 1; Washington, 1883, p. 212.

explorations, to some of the conclusions reached in this connection, as will appear in the chapter devoted to geology and glaciers.

A description of the St. Elias region in the Pacific Coast Pilot supplements the paper in the coast survey report for 1875. This is an exhaustive compilation from all available sources of information interesting to navigators. It contains, besides, a valuable summary of what was known at the time of its publication concerning the history and physical features of the country to which it relates. In this publication the true character of the Malaspina glacier was first recorded and its name proposed. The description is as follows:

"At Point Manby and eastward to the Kwik river the shore was bordered by trees, apparently willows and alders, with a somewhat denser belt a little farther back. Behind this rises a bluff or bank of high land, as described by various navigators. About the vicinity of Tebienkoff's Nearer Point the trees cease, but begin again near the river. The bluff or table-land behind rises higher than the river valley and completely hides it from the southward, and is in summer bare of vegetation (except a few rare patches on its face) and apparently is composed of glacial débris, much of which is of a reddish color. In May, 1874, when observed by the U. S. Coast Survey party of that year, the extensive flattened top of this table-land or plateau was covered with a smooth and even sheet of pure white snow. In the latter part of June, 1880, however, this snow had melted, and for the first time the real and most extraordinary character of this plateau was revealed. Within the beach and extending in a northwesterly direction to the valley behind it, at the foot of the St. Elias Alps an undetermined distance, this plateau, or a large part of it, is one great field of buried ice. Almost everywhere nothing is visible but bowlders, dirt and gravel; but at the time mentioned, back of the bight between Point Manby and Nearer Point, for a space of several square miles the coverlid of dirt had fallen in, owing to the melting of the ice beneath, and revealed a surface of broken pinnacles of ice, each crowned by a patch of dirt, standing close to one another like a forest of prisms, these decreasing in height from the summit of the plateau gradually in a sort of semicircular sweep toward the beach, near which, however, the dirt and débris again predominate, forming a sort of terminal moraine to this immense, buried, immovable glacier, for it is nothing else. Trains of large bowlders were visible here and there, and the general trend of the glacier seemed to be northwest and southeast.

"Between Disenchantment bay and the foot of Mount St. Elias, on the flanks of the Alps, seventeen glaciers were counted, of which about ten were behind this plateau, but none are of very large size, and the sum total of them all seemed far too little to supply the waste of the plateau if it were to possess motion. The lower ends of these small glaciers come down into the river valley before mentioned and at right angles in general to the trend of the plateau. To the buried glacier the U. S. Coast Survey has applied the name of Malaspina, in honor of that distinguished and unfortunate explorer. No connection could be seen between the small glaciers and the Malaspina plateau, as the former dip below the level of the summit of the latter. The Malaspina had no névé, nor was there any high land in the direction of its axis as far as the eye could reach. Everywhere, except where the pinnacles protruded and in a few spots on the face of the bluff, it was covered with a thick stratum of soil, gravel and stones, here and there showing small patches of bright green herbage. The bluff westward from Point Manby may probably prove of the same character."

Mount Cook and Mount Vancouver are named in the Pacific Coast Pilot, and their elevations and positions are definitely stated. Mount Malaspina was also named, but its position is not given. During the expedition of last summer it was found impracticable to decide definitely to which peak the name of the great navigator was applied. So existing nomenclature was followed as nearly as possible by attaching Malaspina's name to a peak about eleven miles east of Mount St. Elias. Its position is indicated on the accompanying map, plate 8 (page 75).

Several charts of the southern coast of Alaska accompany the reports of the United States Coast Survey for 1875, referred to above. A part of these have been independently published. These charts were used in mapping the coast-line as it appears on plate 8, and were frequently consulted while writing the following pages.

NEW YORK TIMES EXPEDITION, 1886.

An expedition sent out by the New York *Times*, in charge of Lieutenant Frederick Schwatka, for the purpose of making geographic explorations and climbing Mount St. Elias, left Sitka on the U. S. S. *Pinta*, on July 10, 1886, and reached Yakutat bay two days later. As it was found impracticable to obtain the necessary assistance from the Indians to continue the voyage to Icy bay, whence the start inland was planned to be made, Captain N. E. Nichols, the commander of the *Pinta*, concluded to take the expedition to its destination in his vessel. On July 17 a landing was made through the surf at Icy bay, and exploration at once began.

The party consisted of Lieutenant Schwatka, in charge; Professor William Libbey, Jr.; and Lieutenant H. W. Seton-Karr.

The camp hands were John Dalton, Joseph Woods, and several Indian packers.*

From Icy bay the expedition proceeded inland, for about sixteen miles, in a line leading nearly due north, toward the summit of Mount St. Elias. The highest point reached, 7,200 feet, was on the foot-hills of the main range now called the Karr hills. The time occupied by the expedition, after leaving Icy bay, was nine or ten days. So far as known, no systematic surveys were carried on.

An interesting account of this expedition appeared in Seton-Karr's book, "The Shores and Alps of Alaska." Many observations on the glaciers and moraines of the region explored are recorded in this work. The map published with it has been used in compiling the western portion of the map forming plate 8, where the route of the expedition is indicated. Another account, especially valuable for its records of scientific observations, by Professor Libbey, was published by the American Geographic Society. The Guyot, Agassiz and Tyndall glaciers, the Chaix hills, and Lake Castani received their names during this expedition.

Lieutenant Schwatka's graphic and entertaining account of this expedition, published in *The Century Magazine* for April, 1891, gives many details of the exploration and illustrates many of the characteristic features of southern Alaska.

Topham Expedition, 1888.

An expedition conducted by Messrs. W. H. and Edwin Topham, of London, George Broka, of Brussels, and William Williams, of New York, was made in 1888. Like the *Times* expedition, it had for its main object the ascent of Mount St. Elias.

Icy bay was reached, by means of canoes from Yakutat bay, on July 13, and an inland journey was made northward which

* The accounts of this expedition are as follows: Report from Lieutenant Schwatka in the New York *Times*, October 17, 1886; Some of the Geographical Features of Southeastern Alaska, by William Libbey, Jr., in Bull. Am. Geog. Soc., 1886, pp. 279–300; Shores and Alps of Alaska, by H. W. Seton Karr, London, 1887, 8°, pp. L–XCV, 142–148; The Alpine Regions of Alaska, by Lieutenant Seton-Karr, in Proc. Roy. Geog. Soc., vol. IX, 1887, pp. 269–285; The Expedition of "The New York Times" (1886), by Lieutenant Schwatka, in *The Century Magazine*, April, 1891, pp. 865–872.

covered a large part of the area traversed by the previous expedition. The highest elevation reached, according to aneroid barometer and boiling-point measurements, was 11,460 feet. This was on the southern side of St. Elias.

The only accounts of this expedition which have come to my notice are an interesting article by William Williams in *Scribner's Magazine,*[*] and a more detailed report by H. W. Topham, accompanied by a map[†] and by a fine illustration of Mount St. Elias, in the Alpine Journal.[‡]

This brief review of explorations carried on in the St. Elias region previous to the expedition sent out in 1890 by the National Geographic Society is incomplete in many particulars,[§] but will indicate the most promising sources of information concerning the country described in the following pages.

* New York, April, 1889, pp. 387–403.

† Topham's map was used in compiling the western portion of the map forming plate 8, and his route is there indicated.

‡ London, August, 1889, pp. 245–371.

§ Yakutat bay has been visited by vessels of the United States Navy and United States Revenue Marine and by numerous trading vessels; but reports of observations made during these voyages have not been found during a somewhat exhaustive search of literature relating to Alaska.

SKETCH MAP OF MOUNT ST. ELIAS REGION, ALASKA

By

Mark B. Kerr.

Western part from maps by H. W. Seton-Karr and W. H. Topham.

Coast line from U.S. Coast Survey.

PART II

NARRATIVE OF THE ST. ELIAS EXPEDITION OF 1890.

ORGANIZATION.

A long-cherished desire to study the geography, geology, and glaciers of the region around Mount St. Elias was finally gratified when, in the summer of 1890, the National Geographic Society made it possible for me to undertake an expedition to that part of Alaska.

The expedition was organized under the joint auspices of the National Geographic Society and the United States Geological Survey, but was greatly assisted by individuals who felt an interest in the extension of geographic knowledge. For the inception of exploration and for securing the necessary funds, credit is due Mr. Willard D. Johnson.

The names of those who subscribed to the exploration fund of the Society are as follows:

Boynton Leach.	Henry Gannett.
Everett Hayden.	Charles J. Bell.
Richardson Clover.	J. S. Diller.
C. M. McCartney.	J. W. Powell.
C. A. Williams.	J. G. Judd.
Willard D. Johnson.	A. Graham Bell.
Israel C. Russell.	Gardiner G. Hubbard.
Gilbert Thompson.	A. W. Greely.
Harry King.	J. W. Dobbins.
Morris Bien.	J. W. Hays.
Wm. B. Powell.	Edmund Alton.
Z. T. Carpenter.	Bailey Willis.
Charles Nordhoff.	E. S. Hosmer.

Rogers Birnie, Jr.

I was chosen by the Board of Managers of the National Geographic Society and by the Director of the United States Geological Survey to take charge of the expedition and to carry on geological and glacial studies. Mr. Mark B. Kerr, topographer on the Geological Survey, was assigned as an assistant, with the duty of making a topographical map of the region explored.

Mr. E. S. Hosmer, of Washington, D. C., volunteered his services as general assistant.*

Mr. Kerr left Washington on May 24 for San Francisco, where he made arrangements for his special work, and reported to me at Seattle on June 15. I left Washington on May 25 and went directly to Seattle, where the necessary preparations for exploring an unknown and isolated region were made.

From the large number of frontiersmen and sailors who applied for positions on the expedition, seven men were selected as camp hands. The foreman of this force was J. H. Christie, of Seattle, who had spent the previous winter in charge of an expedition in the Olympian mountains, and was well versed in all that pertains to frontier life. The other camp hands were J. H. Crumback, L. S. Doney, W. L. Lindsley, William Partridge, Thomas Stamy, and Thomas White.

The individual members of the party will be mentioned frequently during this narrative; but I wish to state at the beginning that very much of the success of the enterprise was due to the hard and faithful work of the camp hands, to each one of whom I feel personally indebted.

Two dogs, "Bud" and "Tweed," belonging to Mr. Christie, also became members of the expedition.

All camp supplies, including tents, blankets, rations, etc., were purchased at Seattle. Rations for ten men for one hundred days, on the basis of the subsistence furnished by the United States Geological Survey, were purchased and suitably packed for transportation in a humid climate. Twenty-five tin cans were obtained, each measuring 6 x 12 x 14 inches, and in each a mixed ration sufficient for one man for fifteen days was packed and hermetically sealed. These rations, thus secured against moisture and in convenient shape for carrying on the back (or "packing"), were for use above the timber line, where cooking was possible only by means of oil stoves. The remainder of the supplies, intended for use where fuel for camp-fires could be obtained, were secured either in tin cans or in canvas sacks.

For cooking above timber line, two double-wick oil stoves were provided, the usual cast-iron bases being replaced by smaller reservoirs of tin, in order to avoid unnecessary weight. Coal oil was carried in five-gallon cans, but a few rectangular cans hold-

* Copies of all instructions governing the work of the expedition are given in Appendix A.

ing one gallon each were provided for use while on the march. Subsequent experience proved that this arrangement was satisfactory.

Four seven-by-seven tents, with ridge ropes, and two pyramidal nine-by-nine center-pole tents, with flies, were provided, all made of cotton drilling. The smaller tents were for use in the higher camps, and the larger ones for the base camps. The tents were as light as seemed practicable, and were found to answer well the purpose for which they were intended.

Each man was supplied with one double Hudson Bay blanket, a water-proof coat, a water-proof hat (the most serviceable being the "sou'westers" used by seamen), and an alpenstock.[*] Each man also carried a sheet made of light duck, seven feet square, to protect his blankets and to be used as a shelter-tent if required. Each member of the party was also required to have heavy boots or shoes, and suitable woolen clothing. Each man was furnished with two pieces of hemp "cod-line," 50 feet in length, to be used in packing blankets and rations. The lines were doubled many times, so as to distribute the weight on the shoulders, and were connected with two leather straps for buckling about the package to be carried. The cod-lines were used instead of ordinary pack-straps, for the reason that they distribute the weight on the shoulder over a broader area, and also because they can be made immediately available for climbing, crossing streams, etc., when required. Several extra lines of the same material were also taken as a reserve, or to be used in roping the party together when necessary. Several of the party carried rifles, for each of which a hundred rounds of fixed ammunition were issued. Two ice-axes for the party were also provided.

A canvas boat was made by the men while en route for the field, but there was no occasion to use it, except as a cover for a cache left at one of the earlier camps. Subsequent experience showed that snow-shoes and one or two sleds would have been serviceable; but these were not taken.

Our instruments were furnished by the United States Geological Survey. The list included one transit, one gradienter, one sextant, two prismatic compasses, one compass clinometer,

---

[*] Light rubber cloth was ordered from San Francisco for the purpose of allowing each man a water-proof sheet to place under his blankets, but was not received in time to be used.

four pocket thermometers, two psychrometers, one field-glass, two mercurial barometers, three aneroids, steel tape-lines, and two photographic outfits.

From Seattle to Sitka.

Preparations having been completed, the expedition sailed from Seattle June 16, on the steamer *Queen*, belonging to the Pacific Coast Steamship Company, in command of Captain James Carroll, and reached Sitka on the morning of June 24. This portion of our voyage was through the justly celebrated " inland passage" of British Columbia and southeastern Alaska, and was in every way delightful. We touched at Victoria and Wrangell, and, after threading the Wrangell narrows, entered Frederick sound, where the first floating ice was seen. The bergs were from a neighboring glacier, which enters the sea at the head of a deep-inlet, too far away to be seen from the course followed by the *Queen*. The route northward led through Stephens passage, and afforded glimpses of glaciers both on the mainland and on Admiralty island. In Taku inlet several hours were spent in examining the glaciers, two of which come down to the sea. One on the western side of the fjord, an ice-stream known as the Norris glacier, descends through a deep valley and expands into a broad ice-foot on approaching the water, though it is not washed by the waves, owing to an accumulation of mud about its extremity. Another ice-stream is the Taku glacier, situated at the head of the inlet. It comes boldly down to the water, and ends in a splendid sea-cliff of azure blue, some 250 feet high. The adjacent waters are covered with icebergs shed by the glacier. Some of the smaller fragments were hoisted on board the *Queen* for table use. The bold, rocky shores of the inlet are nearly bare of vegetation, and indicate by their polished and striated surfaces that glaciers of far greater magnitude than those now existing formerly flowed through this channel.

After leaving Taku inlet, a day was spent at Juneau; and then the *Queen* steamed up Lynn canal to Pyramid harbor, near its head. For picturesque beauty, this is probably the finest of the fjords of Alaska. Several glaciers on each side of the inlet come down nearly to the sea, and all the higher mountains are buried beneath perpetual snow. On returning from Lynn canal, the *Queen* visited Glacier bay, and here passengers were allowed a few hours on shore at the Muir glacier. The day of our visit

was unusually fine, and a splendid view of the great ice-stream
with its many tributaries was obtained from a hill-top about a
thousand feet high, on its eastern border. The glacier discharges
into the head of the bay and forms a magnificent line of ice-
cliffs over two hundred feet high and three miles in extent.

This portion of the coast of Alaska has been described by
several writers; yet its bleak shores are still in large part unexplored. To the west of the bay rise the magnificent peaks of
the Fairweather range, from which flow many great ice-streams.
The largest of the glaciers descending from these mountains into
Glacier bay is called the Pacific glacier. Like the Muir glacier,
it discharges vast numbers of icebergs into the sea.

The day after leaving Glacier bay we arrived at Sitka, and as
soon as practicable called on Lieutenant-Commander O. F.
Farenholt, of the U. S. S. *Pinta*, who had previously received
instructions from the Secretary of the Navy to take us to Yakutat
bay. We also paid our respects to the Governor and other
Alaskan officials, and made a few final preparations for the start
westward.

FROM SITKA TO YAKUTAT BAY.

All of our effects having been transferred to the *Pinta*, we put
to sea early on the morning of June 25.

Honorable Lyman E. Knapp, Governor of Alaska, taking
advantage of the sailing of the *Pinta*, accompanied us on the
voyage. Mr. Henry Boursin, census enumerator, also joined us
for the purpose of obtaining information concerning the Indians
at Yakutat.

The morning we left Sitka was misty, with occasional showers;
but even these unfavorable conditions could not obscure the
beauty of the wild, densely wooded shore along which we steamed.
The weather throughout the voyage was thick and foggy and the
sea rough. We anchored in De Monti bay, the first indentation
on the eastern shore of Yakutat bay, late the following afternoon,
without having obtained so much as a glimpse of the magnificent scenery of the rugged Fairweather range.

At Yakutat we found two small Indian villages, one on Khantaak island and the other on the mainland to the eastward (both
shown on plate 8). The village on Khantaak island is the older
of the two, and consists of six houses built along the water's
edge. The houses are made of planks, each hewn from a single

log, after the manner of the Thlinkets generally. They are rectangular, and have openings in the roofs, with wind guards, for
the escape of smoke. The fires, around which the families
gather, are built in the centers of the spaces below. The houses
are entered by means of oval openings, elevated two feet above
the ground on platforms along their fronts. In the interior of
each there is a rectangular space about twenty feet square surrounded by raised platforms, the outer portions of which are
shut off by partitions and divided into smaller chambers.

The canoes used at Yakutat are each hewn from a single
spruce log, and are good examples of the boats in use throughout
southern Alaska. They are of all sizes, from a small craft
scarcely large enough to hold a single Indian to graceful boats
forty or fifty feet in length and capable of carrying a ton of mer-
chandise with a dozen or more men. They have high, over-
reaching stems and sterns, which give them a picturesque,
gondola-like appearance.

The village on the mainland is less picturesque, if such a term
may be allowed, than the group of houses already described,
but it is of the same type. Near at hand, along the shore to the
southward, there are two log houses, one of which is used at
present as a mission by Reverend Carl J. Hendriksen and his
assistant, the other being occupied as a trading post by Sitka
merchants.

The Yakutat Indians are the most westerly branch of the
great Thlinket family which inhabits all of southeastern Alaska
and a portion of British Columbia. In intelligence they are
above the average of Indians generally, and are of a much higher
type than the native inhabitants of the older portion of the
United States. They are quick to learn the ways of the white
man, and are especially shrewd in bargaining. They are canoe
Indians *par excellence*, and pass a large part of their lives on the
water in quest of salmon, seals, and sea-otter. During the summer of our visit, about thirty sea-otter were taken. They are
usually shot in the primitive manner with copper-pointed arrows,
although repeating rifles of the most improved patterns are
owned by the natives, in spite of existing laws against selling
breech-loading arms to Indians. The fur of the sea-otter is
acknowledged to be the most beautiful, and is the most highly
prized of all pelts. Those taken at Yakutat during our visit
were sold at an average price of about seventy-five dollars. This,

together with the sale of less valuable skins and the money received for baskets, etc., made by the women for the tourist trade in Sitka, brought a considerable revenue to the village. Improvident, like nearly all Indians, the Yakutat villagers soon spend at the trading post the money earned in this way.

The Yakutats belong without question to the Thlinket stock; but visits from tribes farther westward, who travel in skin boats, are known to have been made, and it seems probable that some mixture of Thlinket and Innuit blood may occur in the natives at Yakutat. But if such admixture has occurred, the Innuit element is so small that it escapes the notice of one not skilled in ethnology.

We found Mr. Hendriksen most kind and obliging, and are indebted to him for many favors and great assistance. Arrangements were made with him for reading a base-barometer three times a day during July and August. He also assisted us by acting as an interpreter, and in hiring Indians and canoes.

The weather continued thick and stormy after reaching Yakutat bay, and Captain Farenholt did not think it advisable to take his vessel up the main inlet, where many dangers were reported to exist. A canoe having been purchased from the trader and others hired from the Indians, a start was made from the head of Yakutat bay early on the morning of June 28, in company with two of the *Pinta's* boats loaded with supplies, under the command of Ensign C. W. Jungen.

Canoe Trip up Yakutat Bay.

Bidding good-bye to our friends on the *Pinta*, to whom we were indebted for many favors, we started for our trip up the bay in a pouring rain-storm. Our way at first led through the narrow, placid water-ways dividing the islands on the eastern side of the bay. The islands and the shores of the mainland are densely wooded, and appeared picturesque and inviting even through the veil of mist and rain that shrouded them. The forests consist principally of spruce trees, so dense and having such a tangle of underbrush that it is only with the greatest difficulty that one can force a way through them; while the ground beneath the forest, and even the trunks and branches of the living trees, are covered and festooned with luxuriant growths of mosses and lichens. Our trip along these wooded shores, but half revealed through the drifting mist, was novel and enjoyable in spite of discomforts due to the rain. We rejoiced at the thought that we were nearing the place where the actual labors of the expedition would begin; we were approaching the unknown; visions of unexplored regions filled with new wonders occupied our fancies, and made us eager to press on.

About noon on the first day we pitched our tents on a strip of shingle skirting the shore of the mainland to the east of Knight island. The *Pinta's* boats spread their white wings and sailed away to the southward before a freshening wind, and our last connection with civilization was broken. As one of the frontiersmen of our party remarked, we were "at home once more." It may appear strange to some that any one could apply such a term to a camp on the wild shore of an unexplored country; but the Bohemian spirit is so strong in some breasts, and the restraint of civilization so irksome, that the homing instinct is reversed and leads irresistibly to the wilderness and to the silent mountain tops.

The morning after arriving at our first camp, Kerr, Christie, and Hendriksen, with all the camp hands except two, went on with the canoes, and in a few hours reached the entrance of Disenchantment bay. They found a camping place about twelve miles ahead, on a narrow strip of shingle beneath the precipices of Point Esperanza, and there established our second camp.

My necessary delay at Camp 1 was utilized, so far as possible, in learning what I could concerning the adjacent country, and in making a beginning in the study of its geology. Our camp was at the immediate base of the mountains, and on the northeastern side of the wide plateau bordering the continent. The plateau stretches southeastward for twenty or thirty miles, and is low and heavily forested. The eastern shore of the bay near our first camp is formed of bluffs about 150 feet high, which have been eaten back by the waves so as to expose fine sections of the strata of sand, gravel and bowlders of which the plateau is composed. All the lowlands bordering the mountains have, apparently, a common history, and doubtless owe their origin principally to the deposition of débris brought from the mountains by former glaciers. When this material was deposited, or soon afterward, the land was depressed about 150 feet lower than at present, as is shown by a terrace cut along the base of the mountains at that elevation. The steep mountain face extending northwestward from Camp 1 to the mouth of Disenchantment bay bears evidence of being the upheaved side of a fault of quite recent origin. The steep inclination and shattered condition of the rocks along this line are evidently due to the crushing which accompanied the displacement.

In the wild gorge above our first camp, a small glacier was found descending to within 500 feet of the sea-level, and giving rise to a wild, roaring stream of milky water. Efforts to reach the glacier were frustrated by the density of the dripping vegetation and by the clouds that obscured the mountains.

A canoe trip was made to a rocky islet between Knight island and the mainland toward the north. The islet, like the rocks in the adjacent mountain range, is composed of sandstone, greatly shattered and seamed, and nearly vertical in attitude. Its surface was densely carpeted with grass and brilliant flowers. Many sea birds had their homes there. From its summit a fine view was obtained of the cloud-capped mountains toward the northeast, of the dark forest covering Knight island, and of the broad plateau toward the southeast. Some of the most charming effects in the scenery of the forest-clad and mist-covered shores of Alaska are due to the wreaths of vapor ascending from the deep forests during the interval in which the warm sunlight shines through the clouds; and on the day of our visit to the islet, the forests, when not concealed by mist, sent up smoke-like vapor wreaths of many fantastic shapes to mingle with the clouds in which the higher mountains disappeared.

At Camp 1 the personnel of the party was unexpectedly reduced. Mr. Hosmer was ill, and remained with me at camp instead of pushing on with Kerr and Christie; and the weather continuing stormy, he concluded to abandon the expedition and return to the mission at Port Mulgrave. Having secured the services of an Indian who chanced to pass our camp in his canoe, Mr. Hosmer bade us good-bye, ensconced himself in the frail craft, and started for sunnier lands. It was subsequently learned that he reached Yakutat without mishap, and a few days later sailed for Sitka in a small trading schooner. Our force during the remainder of the season, not including Mr. Hendriksen and the Indians, whose services were engaged for only a few days, numbered nine men all told.

On the evening of June 30 we had a bright camp-fire blazing on the beach to welcome the returning party. Near sunset a canoe appeared in the distance, and a shot was fired as it came round a bend in the shore. We felt sure that our companions were returning, and piled drift-wood on the roaring camp-fire to cheer them after their hard day's work on the water. As the canoe approached, each dip of the paddle sent a flash of light to us, and we could distinguish the men at their work; but we soon discovered that it was occupied not by our own party but by Indians returning from a seal hunt in Disenchantment bay. They brought their canoe high on the beach, and made themselves at home about our camp-fire. There were seven or eight well-built young men in the party, all armed with guns. In former times such an arrival would have been regarded with suspicion; but thanks to the somewhat frequent visits of war vessels to Yakutat, and also to the labors of missionaries, the wild spirits of the Indians have been greatly subdued and reduced to semi-civilized condition during the past quarter of a century.

Just as the long twilight deepened into night, another craft came around the distant headland, but less swiftly than the former one; and soon our picturesque canoe, with Christie at the stern steering with a paddle in true Indian fashion, grated on the shingle beach. Christie has spent many years of his life with the Indians of the Northwest, and has adopted some of their habits. On beginning frontier life once more, he discarded the hat of the white man, and wore a blue cloth tied tightly around his forehead and streaming off in loose ends behind. The change was welcome, for it added to the picturesque appearance of the party.

The men, weary with their long row against currents and head-winds, greatly enjoyed the camp-fire. Our Indian visitors, after lunching lightly on the leaf-stalks of a plant resembling celery (*Archangelica*), which grows abundantly everywhere on the lowlands of southern Alaska, departed toward Yakutat. Supper was served in one of the large tents, and we all rolled ourselves in our blankets for the night.

The next day, July 1, we abandoned Camp 1, passed by Camp 2, and late in the afternoon reached the northwestern side of Yakutat bay, opposite Point Esperanza. Our trip along the wild shore, against which a heavy surf was breaking, was full of novelty and interest. The mountains rose sheer from the water to a height of two or three thousand feet. About their bases, like dark drapery, following all the folds of the mountain side, ran a band of vegetation; but the spruce forests had mostly disappeared, and only a few trees were seen here and there in the deeper cañons. The position of the terrace along the base of the mountain, first noticed at Camp 1, could be plainly traced, although densely covered with bushes. The mountain peaks above were all sharp and angular, indicating at a glance that they had never been subjected to glacial action. The sandstone and shales forming the naked cliffs are fractured and crushed, and are evidently yielding rapidly to the weather; but the characteristic red color due to rock decay could not be seen. The prevailing tone of the mountains, when not buried beneath vegetation or covered with snow, is a cold gray. Bright, warm, summer skies are needed to reveal the variety and beauty of that forbidding region.

Our large canoe behaved well, although heavily loaded. Sometimes the wind was favorable, when an extemporized sail lessened the fatigue of the trip. The landing on the northwestern shore was effected, through a light surf, on a sandy beach heavily encumbered with icebergs. As it was hazardous to beach the large canoe with its load of boxes and bags, the heavy freight was transferred, a few pieces at a time, to smaller canoes, each manned by a single Indian, and all was safely landed beyond the reach of the breakers. Camp 3 was established on the sandy beach just above the reach of the tide and near the mouth of a roaring brook. The drift-wood along the shore furnished abundant fuel for a blazing camp-fire; our tents were pitched, and once more we felt at home.

Two canoes were dispatched, in care of Doney, to the camp on the opposite shore (Camp 2), with instructions to bring over the equipments left there. Kerr went over also for the purpose of making a topographic station on the bluff forming Point Esperanza should the morrow's weather permit.

It was curious to note the care which our Indians took of their canoes. Not only were they drawn high up on the beach, out of the reach of all possible tides, but each canoe was swathed in wet cloths, especially at the prow and stern, to prevent them from drying and cracking. The canoes, being fashioned from a single spruce log, are especially liable to split if allowed to dry thoroughly.

The day after our arrival, all of our party and all of our camp

outfit were assembled at Camp 3. Mr. Hendrickson and our
Indian friends took their departure, and the work for which we
had come so far was actually begun.

Base Camp on the Shore of Yakutat Bay.

About the tents at Camp 3 the rank grass grew waist-high,
sheltering the strawberries and dwarf raspberries that bloomed
beneath. A little way back from the shore, clumps of alders, in-
terspersed with spruce trees, marked the beginning of the forest
which covered the hills toward the west and southwest. Toward
the north rose rugged mountains, their summits shrouded in
mist; in the steep gorges on their sides the ends of glaciers
gleamed white, like foaming cataracts descending from cloudland.

The day following our arrival dawned bright and beautiful.
Every cloud vanished from the mountains as by magic, reveal-
ing their magnificent summits in clear relief. We found ourselves at the base of a rugged mountain range extending far
southeastward and northwestward, its first rampart so breached
as to allow the waters of the ocean to extend into the very midst
of the great peaks beyond. Through this opening we had a
splendid view of the snow-clad mountains filling the northern
sky and stretching away in lessening perspective toward the
east until they blended with the distant clouds.

Topographic work was started, and the preparation of "packs"
for the journey inland was begun at once; and all hands were
kept busy. A base-line was measured by Mr. Kerr, and a beginning was made in the development of a system of triangulation which was carried on throughout the season.

Our stay at the camp on the shore extended over a week, and
enabled us to become familiar with many of the changes in the
rugged scenery surrounding Yakutat bay. The bay itself was
covered with icebergs for most of the time. Owing to the prevailing winds and the action of shore currents, the ice accumulated on the coast adjacent to our camp. For many days the
beach toward both the north and the south, as far as the eye
could reach, was piled high with huge masses of blue and white
ice. When the bay was rough, the surf roared angrily among
the stranded bergs and, dashing over them, formed splendid
sheets of form; while on bright, sunny days the bay gleamed
and flashed in the sunlight as the summer winds gently rippled

its surface, and the thousands of icebergs crowding the azure plain seemed a numberless fleet of fairy boats with crystal hulls and fantastic sails of blue and white. When the long summer days drew to a close and gave place to the soft northern twilight, which in summer lasts until the glow of the returning sun is seen in the east, the sea and mountains assumed a soft, mysterious beauty never realized by dwellers in more southern climes. The hours of twilight were so enchanting, the varying shades and changing tints on the mighty snow-fields robing the mountains were so exquisite in their gradations that, even when weary with many hours of toil, the explorer could not resist the charm, and paced the sandy shore until the night was far spent. Sometimes in the twilight hours, long after the sun disappeared, the summits of the majestic peaks toward the east were transformed by the light of the after-glow into mountains of flame. As the light faded, the cold shadow of the world crept higher and higher up the crystal slopes until only the topmost spires and pinnacles were gilded by the sunset glow. At such times, when our eyes were weary with watching the gorgeous transformation of the snow-covered mountains and were turned to the far-reaching seaward view, we would be startled by the sight of a vast city, with battlements, towers, minarets, and domes of fantastic architecture, rising where we knew that only the berg-covered waters extended. The appearance of these phantom cities was a common occurrence during the twilight hours. Although we knew at once that the ghostly spires were but a trick of the mirage, yet their ever-changing shapes and remarkable mimicry of human habitations were so striking that they never lost their novelty; and they were never the same on two successive evenings. One of the most common deceptions of the mirage is the transformation of icebergs into the semblance of fountains gushing from the sea and expanding into graceful, sheaf-like shapes. The strangest freaks due to the refraction of light on hot deserts, which are usually supposed to be the home of the mirage, do not excite the traveler's wonder so much as the phantom cities seen in the uncertain twilight amid the ice-packs of the north.

When the slowly deepening twilight transformed mountains and seas into a dreamland picture, the harvest moon, strangely out of place in far northern skies, spread a sheet of silver behind the dark headlands toward the southeast, and then slowly appeared, not rising boldly toward the zenith, but tracing a low arch in the southern heavens, to soon disappear into the sea toward the southwest. Brief as were her visits, they were always welcome and always brought the feeling that distant homes were nearer when the same light was visible to us and to loved ones far away. The soft moonlight dimmed the twilight, the after-glow faded from the highest peaks, and the short northern night came on.

After returning from the mountains, late in September, we were again encamped on the northwestern shore of Yakutat bay. A heavy northeast storm swept down from the mountains and awakened all the pent-up fury of the waves. The beach was crowded with bergs, among which the surf broke in great sheets of feathery foam; clouds of spray were dashed far above the icy ramparts, carrying with them fragments of ice torn from the bergs over which they swept; while the stranded bergs rocked violently to and fro as the waves burst over them. Sometimes the raging waters, angered by opposition, lifted the bergs in their mighty arms and, turning them over and over, dashed them high on the beach. It seemed as if spirits of the deep, unable to leave the water-world, were hurling their weapons at unseen enemies on the land. The fearful grandeur of the raging waters and of the dark storm-swept skies was, perhaps, enhanced by the fact that the landward-blowing gale, combined with a rising tide, threatened to sweep away our frail home. Each succeeding wave, as it rolled shoreward, sent a sheet of foam roaring and rushing up the beach and creeping nearer and nearer to our shelter until only a few inches intervened between the high-water line and the crest of the sand bank that protected us. The limit was reached at last, however, and the water slowly re-treated, leaving a fringe of ice within arm's length of our tents.

The wild scene along the shore was especially grand at night. The stranded bergs, seen through the gloom, formed strange moving shapes, like vessels in distress. The white banners of spray seemed signals of disaster. An Armada, more numerous than ever sailed from the ports of Spain, was being crushed and ground to pieces by the hoarse wind and raging surf. Sleep was impossible, even if one cared to rest when sea and air and sky were joined in fierce conflict. Our tents, spared by the waves, were dashed down by the fierce north winds, and a lake in the forest toward the west overflowed its banks and discharged its flooding waters through our encampment. At last, tired and discomforted, we abandoned our tents and retreated to the neighboring forest and there took refuge in a cabin built near where a coal seam outcrops, and remained until the storm had spent its force. But I have anticipated, and must return to the thread of my narrative.

First Day's Tramp.

The impressions received during the first day spent on shore in a new country are always long remembered. Of several "first days" in my own calendar, there are none that exceed in interest my first excursions through the forest and over the hills west of Yakutat bay.

Every one about camp having plenty of work to occupy him through the day, I started out early on the morning of July 2, with only "Bud" and "Tweed" for companions. My objects were to reconnoiter the country to the westward, to learn what I could concerning its geology and glaciers, and to choose a line of march toward Mount St. Elias.

To the north of our camp, and about a mile distant, rose a densely wooded hill about 300 feet high, with a curving outline, convex southward. This hill had excited my curiosity on first catching sight of the shore, and I decided to make it my first study. Its position at the mouth of a steep gorge in the hills beyond, down which a small glacier flowed, suggested that it might be an ancient moraine, deposited at a time when the ice-stream advanced farther than at present. My surprise therefore was great when, after forcing my way through the dense thickets, I reached the top of the hill, and found a large kettle-shaped depression, the sides of which were solid walls of ice fifty feet high. This showed at once that the supposed hill was really the extremity of a glacier, long dead and deeply buried beneath forest-covered débris. In the bottom of the kettle-like depression lay a pond of muddy water, and, as the ice-cliffs about the lakelet melted in the warm sunlight, miniature avalanches of ice and stones, mingled with sticks and bushes that had been undermined, frequently rattled down its sides and splashed into the waters below. Further examination revealed the fact that scores of such kettles are scattered over the surface of the buried glacier. This ice-stream is that designated the *Galiano glacier* on the accompanying map.

Continuing on my way toward the mouth of the gorge in the

mountains above. I forced my way for nearly a mile through dense thickets, frequently making wide detours to avoid the kettle holes. At length the vegetation became less dense, and gave place to broad open fields of rocks and dirt, covering the glacier from side to side. This débris was clearly of the nature of a moraine, as the ice could be seen beneath it in numerous crevasses; but no division into marginal or medial moraines could be distinguished. It is really a thin, irregular sheet of comminuted rock, together with angular masses of sandstone and shale, the largest of which are ten or fifteen feet in diameter. When seen from a little distance the débris completely conceals the ice and forms a barren, rugged surface, the picture of desolation.

After traversing this naked area the clear ice in the center of the gorge was reached. All about were wild cliffs, stretching up toward the snow-covered peaks above; several cataracts of ice, formed by tributary glaciers descending through rugged, highly inclined channels, were in sight ; while the snow-fields far above gleamed brilliantly in the sunlight, and now and then sent down small avalanches to awaken the echoes of the cliffs and fill the still air with a Babel of tongues.

Pushing on toward the western border of the glacier, across the barren field of stones, I came at length to the brink of a precipice of dirty ice more than a hundred feet high, at the foot of which flowed a swift stream of turbid water. A few hundred yards below, this stream suddenly disappeared beneath an archway formed by the end of a glacial tunnel, and its further course was lost to view. It was a strange sight to see a swift, foaming river burst from beneath overhanging ice-cliffs, roar along over a bowlder-covered bed, and then plunge into the mouth of a cavern, leaving no trace of its lower course except a dull, heavy rumbling far down below the icy surface. A still grander example of these glacial streams, observed a few days later, is described on another page.

The bank of the gulf opposite the point at which I first reached it is formed by a steep mountain-side supporting a dense growth of vegetation. Here and there, however, streams of water plunge down the slope, making a chain of foaming cascades, and opening the way through the vegetation. It seemed practicable to traverse one of these stream beds without great difficulty, and thus to reach the plateau which I knew, from a more distant view, to exist above.

Crossing the glacial river above the upper archway, I reached the mountain side and began to ascend. The task was far more difficult than anticipated. The bushes, principally of alder and currant, grew dense and extended their branches down the steep slope in such a manner that at times it was utterly impossible to force a way through them. Much of the way I crawled on hands and knees up the steep watercourse beneath the dense tangle of vegetation overhanging from either bank and interlacing in the center. On nearing the top I was so fortunate as to strike a bear trail, along which the animal had forced his way through the bushes, making an opening like a tunnel. Through this I ascended to the top of the slope, coming out in a wild amphitheatre in the side of the mountain. The bottom of the amphitheatre was exceedingly rough, owing to confused moraine-heaps, and held a number of small lakes. On account of its elevation, it was not densely covered with bushes, and no trees were in sight except along its southern margin. About its northern border ran a broad terrace, marking the height of the great glacier which formerly occupied the site of Yakutat bay. The terrace formed a convenient pathway leading westward to a sharp ridge running out from the mountains and connecting with an outstanding butte, which promised to afford an unobstructed view to the westward.

Pressing on, I found that the terrace on which I was traveling at length became a free ridge, some three hundred feet high, with steep slopes on either side, like a huge railroad embankment. This ridge swept across the valley in a graceful curve, and shut off a portion of the western part of the amphitheatre from the general drainage. In the portion thus isolated there was a lake without an outlet, still frozen. The snow banks bordering the frozen lake were traced in every direction by the trails of bears. Continuing my tramp, I crossed broad snow-fields, climbed the ridge to the westward, and obtained a far-reaching, unobstructed view of the surrounding country. The elevation reached was only about 1,500 feet above sea-level, but was above the timber line. The mountain slopes toward the north were bare of vegetation and generally covered with snow.

The first object to claim attention was the huge pyramid forming the summit of Mount St. Elias, which stood out clear and sharp against the northwestern sky. Although thirty-six miles distant, it dominated all other peaks in view and rose far above the rugged crests of nearer ranges, many of which would have been counted magnificent mountains in a less rugged land. This was the first view of the great peak obtained by any of our party. Not a cloud obscured the delineation of the mountain; and the wonderful transparency of the atmosphere, after so many days of mist and rain, was something seldom if ever equalled in less humid lands.

Much nearer than St. Elias, and a little west of north of my station, rose Mount Cook, one of the most beautiful peaks in the region. Its summit, unlike the isolated pyramid in which St. Elias terminates, is formed of three white domes, with here and there subordinate pinnacles of pure white, shooting up from the snow-fields like great crystals. On the southern side of Mount Cook there are several rugged and angular ridges, which sweep away for many miles and project like headlands into the sea of ice, known as the Malaspina glacier, bordering the ocean toward the southwest. Between the main ridges there are huge trunk glaciers, each contributing its flood of ice to the great glacier below; and each secondary valley and each amphitheatre among the peaks, no matter how small, has its individual glacier, and the majority of these are tributary to the larger ice-streams. All the mountains in sight exceeding 2,000 feet in elevation were white with snow, except the sharpest ridges and boldest precipices. The attention of the geologist is attracted by the fact that all the foot-hills of Mount Cook are composed of gray sandstone and black shale; and he also observes that the angular mountain crest so sharply drawn against the sky furnishes abundant evidence that the mountains were never subjected to the abrasion of a continuous ice-sheet.

As I stood on the steep-sloped ridge, the Atrevida and Lucia glaciers, their surfaces covered from side to side with angular masses of sandstone and shale, lay at my feet; while farther up the valley the débris on the surface of the ice disappeared, and all above was a winter landscape. The brown, desolate débris-fields on the glacier at my feet extended far southward, and covered the expanded ice-foot in which the glacier terminates. Most curious of all was the fact that the moraines on the lower border of the glacier were concealed from view by a dense covering of vegetation, and in places were clothed with forests of spruce trees.

To the southward, beyond the end of the Lucia glacier, and separated from it by a torrent-swept bowlder-bed, lay a vast plateau of ice which stretched toward the south and west farther than the eye could reach. This is the Malaspina glacier, shown on plate 8. Its borders, like the expanded extremity of the Lucia glacier, are covered with débris, on the outer margins of which dense vegetation has taken root. All the central portion of the ice-sheet is clear of moraines, and shone in the sunlight like a vast snow-field. The heights formerly reached by the nearer glaciers were plainly marked along the mountain sides by well-defined terraces, sloping with the present drainage. When the Lucia glacier was at its flood the ridge on which I stood was only 200 or 300 feet above its surface; now it approaches 1,000 feet.

Turning toward the southeast, I could look down upon the waters of Yakutat bay, with its thousands of floating icebergs, and could distinguish the white breakers as they rolled in on Ocean cape. Beyond Yakutat stretches a forest-covered plateau between the mountains and the sea, and the eye could range far over the mountains bordering this plateau on the northeast. In the distance, fully a hundred miles away, stood Mount Fairweather, its position rendered conspicuous by a bank of shining clouds floating serenely above its cold summit.

The mountains directly east of Yakutat bay rise to a general height of about 8,000 feet, but are without especially prominent peaks. In a general way they form a rugged plateau, which has been dissected in various channels to depth of 2,000 or 3,000 feet. Nearly all of the plateau, including mountains and valleys, is covered with snow-fields and glaciers; but none of the ice-streams, so far as can be seen from a distance, descend below an elevation of about 4,000 or 5,000 feet. This region is as yet untraversed; and when the explorer enters it, it is quite possible that deep drainage lines will be found through which glaciers may descend nearly or quite to sea-level.

After drinking in the effect of the magnificent landscape and endeavoring to impress every detail in the rugged topography upon my memory, and having finished writing my notes, it was time to return; for the sun was already declining toward the west. Wishing to see more of the wonderful land about me, I concluded to descend the western slope of the ridge upon which I stood, and to return to camp by following a stream which issues from the Atrevida glacier directly below my station and empties into Yakutat bay a mile or two south of our third camp.

The quickest and easiest way down was to slide on the snow. Using my alpenstock as a brake, I descended swiftly several hundred feet without difficulty, the dogs bounding along beside me, when on looking up I was startled to see two huge brown bears on the same snow surface, a little to the left and not more than a hundred and fifty yards away. Had my slide been continued a few seconds more I should have been in exceedingly unwelcome company. I was unarmed, and entirely unprepared for a fight with two of the most savage animals found in this country. The bears had long yellowish-brown hair, and were of the size and character of the "grizzly," with which they are thought by hunters, if not by naturalists, to be specifically identical. They were not at all disturbed by my presence, and in spite of my shouts, which I thought would make them travel off, one of them came leisurely toward me. His strides over the snow revealed a strength and activity commanding admiration despite the decidedly uncomfortable feeling awakened by his proximity and evident curiosity. Later in the season I measured the tracks of an animal of the same species, made while walking over a soft, level surface, and found each impression to measure 9 by 17 inches, and the stride to reach 64 inches. So far as I have been able to learn, this is the largest bear track that has been reported. Realizing my danger, I continued my snow slide, but in a different direction and with accelerated speed. The upper limit of the dense thicket clothing the slope of the mountain was soon reached, and my unwelcome companions were lost to sight.

Following the bed of a torrent fed by the snow-fields above, I soon came to the creek chosen for my route back to camp; the waters, brown and turbid with sediment, welled out of a cavern at the foot of an ice precipice 200 feet high, and formed a roaring stream too deep and too swift for fording. The roaring of the brown waters and the startling noises made by stones rattling down the ice-cliff, together with the dark shadows of the deep gorge, walled in by a steep mountain slope on one side and a glacier on the other, made the route seem uncanny. On the sands filling the spaces between the bowlders there were many fresh bear tracks, which at least suggested that the belated traveler should be careful in his movements.

This locality was afterward occupied as a camping place, and is shown in the picture forming plate 10. The dark-colored ice,

mixed with stones and earth, might easily be mistaken for stratified rock: but the dirt discoloring the ice is almost entirely super-
ficial. The crest of the cliff is formed of débris, and is the edge
of the sheet of stones and earth covering the general surface of
the glacier. Owing to the constant melting, stones and bowlders
are continually loosened to rattle down the steep slope and plunge
into the water beneath.

I followed down the bank of the stream, by springing from
bowlder to bowlder, for about a mile, and then came to a steep
bluff, the western side of which was swept by the roaring flood.
The banks above were clothed with spruce trees and dense underbrush; but, there being no alternative, I entered the forest and
slowly worked my way in the direction of camp. To traverse
the unbroken forests of southern Alaska is always difficult, even
when one is fresh; and, weary as I was with many hours of
laborious climbing, my progress was slow indeed. One of the
principal obstacles encountered in threading these Arctic jungles
is the plant known as the "Devil's club" (*Panax horridum*), which
grows to a height of ten or fifteen feet, and has broad, palmate
leaves that are especially conspicuous in autumn, owing to their
bright yellow color. The stems of this plant run on the earth
for several feet and then curve upward. Every portion of its
surface, even to the ribs of the leaves, is thickly set with spines,
which inflict painful wounds, and, breaking off in the flesh,
cause festering sores. In forcing a way through the brush one
frequently treads on the prostrate portion of these thorny plants,
and not infrequently is made aware of the fact by a blow on the
head or in the face from the over-arching stems.

I struggled on through the tangled vegetation until the sun
went down and the woods became dark and somber. Thick
moss, into which the foot sank as in a bed of sponge, covered
the ground everywhere to the depth of two or three feet; each
fallen trunk was a rounded mound of green and brown, decked
with graceful equiseta and ferns, or brilliant with flowers, but
most treacherous and annoying to the belated traveler. In the
gloom of the dim-lit woods, the trees, bearded with moss, assumed strange, fantastic shapes, which every unfamiliar sound
seemed to start into life; while the numerous trails made by the
bears in forcing their way through the thick tangle were positive evidence that not all the inhabitants of the forest were creatures of the imagination. My faithful companions, "Bud" and

"Tweed" showed signs of weariness, and offered no objection when I started a fire and expressed my intention of spending the night beneath the wide-spreading branches of a moss-covered evergreen. Having a few pieces of bread in my pocket, I shared them with the dogs, and stretching myself on a luxuriant bank of lichens tried to sleep, only to find the mosquitoes so energetic that there was no hope of passing the night in comfort.

After resting I felt refreshed, and concluded to press on through the gathering darkness, and after another hour of hard work I came out of the forest and upon a field of torrent-swept bowlders, deposited by the stream which I had left farther up. I was surprised to find that the twilight was not so far spent as I had fancied. The way ahead being free of vegetation, I hastened on, and after traveling about two miles was rejoiced by the sight of a camp-fire blazing in the distance. The warm fire and a hearty supper soon made me forget the fatigues of the day.

This, my first day's exploration, must stand as an example of many similar days spent on the hills and in the forests northwest of Yakutat bay, of which it is not necessary to give detailed descriptions.

Canoe Trip in Disenchantment Bay.

On July 3, I continued my examination of the region about the head of Yakutat bay by making a canoe trip up Disenchantment bay to Haenke island. With the assistance of Christie and Crumback, our canoe was launched through the surf without difficulty, and we slowly worked our way through the fields of floating ice which covered all the upper portion of the inlet. The men plied the oars with which the canoe was fortunately provided, while I directed its course with a paddle. A heavy swell rolling in from the ocean rendered the task of choosing a route through the grinding ice-pack somewhat difficult. After four or five hours of hard work, during which time several vain attempts were made to traverse leads in the ice which had only one opening, we succeeded in reaching the southern end of the island.

The shores of Haenke island are steep and rocky, and, so far as I am aware, afford only one cove in which a boat can take refuge. This is at the extreme southern point, and is not visible until its entrance is reached. A break or fissure in the rocks there admits of the accumulation of stone and sand, and this has been extended by the action of the waves and tides until a beach a hundred feet in length has been deposited. The dashing of the bowlders and sand against the cliffs at the head of the cove by the incoming waves has increased its extension in that direction so as to form a well-sheltered refuge. The absence of beaches on other portions of the island is due to the fact that its bordering precipices descend abruptly into deep water, and do not admit of the accumulation of débris about their bases. Without stones and sand with which the waves can work, the excavation of terraces is an exceedingly slow operation. The precipitous nature of the borders of the island is due, to some extent at least, to the abrasion of the rocks by the glacial ice which once encircled it.

Pulling our canoe far up on the beach, we began the ascent of the cliffs. Hundreds of sea birds, startled from their nests by our intrusion, circled fearlessly about our heads and filled the air with their wild cries. The more exposed portions of the slopes were bare of vegetation, but in the shelter of every depression dense thickets obstructed the way. Many of the little basins between the rounded knolls hold tarns of fresh water, and were occupied at the time of our visit by flocks of gray geese. It is evident that the island was intensely glaciated at no distant day. The surfaces of its rounded domes are so smoothly polished that they glitter like mirrors in the sunlight. On the polished surfaces there are deep grooves and fine, hair-like lines, made by the stones set in the bottom of the glacier which once flowed over the island and removed all of the rocks that were not firm and hard. On many of the domes of sandstone there rest bowlders of a different character, which have evidently been brought from the mountains toward the northeast.

The summit of the island is about 800 feet above the level of the sea, and, like its sides, is polished and striated. The terraces on the mountains of the mainland show that the glacier which formerly flowed out from Disenchantment bay must have been fully 2,000 feet deep. The bed it occupied toward the south is now flooded by the waters of Yakutat bay.

At the time of Malaspina's visit, 100 years ago, the glaciers from the north reached Haenke island, and surrounded it on three sides.* At the rate of retreat indicated by comparing

* The map accompanying Malaspina's report and indicating these conditions has already been mentioned, and is reproduced on plate 7, page 68.

Malaspina's records with the present condition, the glaciers must have reached Point Esperanza, at the mouth of Disenchantment bay, about 20 years ago: and an allowance of between 500 and 1,000 years would seem ample for the retreat of the glaciers since they were at their flood.

Reaching the topmost dome of Haenke island, a wonderful panorama of snow-covered mountains, glaciers, and icebergs lay before us. The island occupies the position of the stage in a vast amphitheatre; the spectators are hoary mountain peaks, each a monarch robed in ermine and bidding defiance to the ceaseless war of the elements. How insignificant the wanderer who confronts such an audience, and how weak his efforts to describe such a scene!

From a wild cliff-enclosed valley toward the north, guarded by towering pinnacles and massive cliffs, flows a great glacier, the fountains of which are far back in the heart of the mountains beyond the reach of vision. Having vainly sought an Indian name for this ice-stream, I concluded to christen it the *Dalton glacier*, in honor of John Dalton, a miner and frontiersman now living at Yakutat, who is justly considered the pioneer explorer of the region. The glacier is greatly shattered and pinnacled in descending its steep channel, and on reaching the sea it expands into a broad ice-foot. The last steep descent is made just before gaining the water, and is marked by crevasses and pinnacles of magnificent proportion and beautiful color. This is one of the few glaciers in the St. Elias region that has well-defined medial and lateral moraines. At the bases of the cliffs on the western side there is a broad, lateral moraine, and in the center, looking like a winding road leading up the glacier, runs a triple-banded ribbon of débris, forming a typical medial moraine. The morainal material carried by the glacier is at last deposited at its foot, or floated away by icebergs, and scattered far and wide over the bottom of Yakutat bay.

The glacier expands on entering the water, as is the habit of all glaciers when unconfined, and ends in magnificent ice-cliffs some two miles in length. The water dashing against the bases of the cliffs dissolves them away, and the tides tend to raise and lower the expanded ice-foot. The result is that huge masses, sometimes reaching from summit to base of the cliffs, are undermined, and topple over into the sea with a tremendous crash. Owing to the distance of the glacier from Haenke island, we could

see the fall long before the roar reached our ears; the cliffs separated, and huge masses seemed to sink without a sound; the
spray thrown up as the blue pinnacles disappeared ascended
like gleaming rockets, sometimes as high as the tops of the cliffs,
and then fell back in silent cataracts of foam. Then a noise as
of a cannonade came rolling across the waters and echoing from
cliff to cliff. The roar of the glacier continues all day when the
air is warm and the sun bright, and is most active when the summer days are finest. Sometimes, roar succeeded roar, like artil-
lery fire, and the salutes were answered, gun for gun, by the great
Hubbard glacier, which pours its flood of ice into the fjord a few
miles further northeastward. This ice-stream, most magnificent
of the tide-water glaciers of Alaska yet discovered, and a towering
mountain peak from which the glacier receives a large part of its
drainage, were named in honor of Gardiner G. Hubbard, presi-
dent of the National Geographic Society.

Looking across the waters of the bay, whitened by thousands
of floating bergs, we could see three miles of the ice-cliffs formed
where the Hubbard glacier enters the sea. A dark headland on
the shore of the mainland to the right shut off the full view of
the glacier but formed a strongly drawn foreground, which enhanced the picturesque effect of the scenery. The Hubbard
glacier flows majestically through a deep valley leading back
into the mountains, and has two main branches, with a smaller
and steeper tributary between. These branches unite to form
a single ice-foot extending into the bay. The western branch
has a dark medial moraine down its center, which makes a bold,
sweeping curve before joining the main stream. There is also a
broad lateral débris-belt along the bases of the cliffs forming its
right bank. The whole surface of the united glacier, and all of
the white tongues running back into the mountains beyond the
reach of vision, are broken and shattered, owing to the steepness
and roughness of the bed over which they flow. The surface,
where not concealed by morainal material, is snow-white; but
in the multitude of crevasses the blue ice is exposed, and gives
a greenish-blue tint to the entire stream. Where the subglacial
slopes are steep, the ice is broken into pinnacles and towers of
the grandest description.

On the steep mountain sides sloping toward the Hubbard
glacier there are more than a dozen secondary ice-streams which
are tributary to it. The amphitheatres in which the glacier has

its beginnings have never been seen ; but our general knowledge of the fountains from which glaciers flow assures us that not only scores but hundreds of other secondary and tertiary glaciers far back into the mountains contribute their floods to the same great stream.

After being received on board the *Corwin*, late in September, we had an opportunity to view the great sea-cliffs of the Hubbard glacier near at hand. Captain Hooper, attracted by the magnificent scenery, took his vessel up Disenchantment bay to a point beyond Haenke island, whence a view could be had of the eastern extension of the inlet. So far as is known, the *Corwin* was the first vessel to navigate those waters. Soundings made between the island and the ice-foot gave forty to sixty fathoms. At the elbow, where the southeastern shore of the bay turns abruptly eastward, there is a low islet not represented on any map previous to the one made by the recent expedition, which commands even a wider prospect than can be obtained from Haenke island. Future visitors to this remote coast should endeavor to reach this islet, after having beheld the grand panorama obtainable from the summit of Haenke island. The portion of Disenchantment bay stretching eastward from the foot of Hubbard glacier is enclosed on all sides by bold mountains, the lower slopes of which have the subdued and flowing outlines characteristic of glaciated regions. Several glaciers occur in the high-grade lateral valleys opening from the bay ; but these have recently retreated, and none of them have sufficient volume at present to reach the water. The general recession, in which all the glaciers of Alaska are participating, is manifested here by the broad débris fields, which cover all the lower ice-streams not ending in the sea. The absence of vegetation on the smooth rocks recently abandoned by the ice also tells of recent climatic changes.

A débris-covered glacier, so completely concealed by continuous sheets of stones and earth that its true character can scarcely be recognized, descends from the mountains just east of Hubbard glacier. It is formed by the union of two principal tributaries, and, on reaching comparatively level ground, expands into a broad ice-foot, but does not have sufficient volume to reach the sea. Another glacier, of smaller size but of the same general character, lies between the Hubbard and Dalton glaciers.

In a rugged defile in the mountains just west of Haenke island there is another small dirt-covered glacier, which creeps down from the precipices above and reaches within a mile of the water.

HUBBARD GLACIER

At its end there is a cliff of black, dirty ice, scarcely to be distinguished from rock at a little distance, from the base of which flows a turbid stream. This glacier is covered so completely with earth and stones that not a vestige of the ice can be seen unless we actually traverse its surface. Its appearance suggests the name of *Black glacier*, by which it is designated on the accompanying map.

The visitor to Haenke island has examples of at least two well-marked types of glaciers in view: The small débris-covered ice-streams, too small to reach the water, are typical of a large class of glaciers in southern Alaska, which are slowly wasting away and have become buried beneath débris concentrated at the surface by reason of their own melting. The Galiano glacier is a good example of this class. The Hubbard and Dalton glaciers are fine examples of another class of ice-streams which flow into the sea and end in ice-cliffs, and which for convenience we call *tide-water glaciers*. Nowhere can finer or more beautiful examples of this type be found than those in view from Haenke island.

FIGURE 1—*Diagram illustrating the Formation of Icebergs.*

The formation of icebergs from the undermining and breaking down of the ice-cliffs of the tide-water glaciers has already been mentioned. But there is another method by which bergs are formed—a process even more remarkable than the avalanches that occur when portions of the ice-cliffs topple over into the sea. The ice-cliffs at the foot of the tide-water glaciers are really sea-cliffs formed by the waves cutting back a terrace in the ice. The submerged terrace is composed of ice, and may extend out a thousand feet or more in front of the visible part of the ice-cliffs. These conditions are represented in the accompanying diagram (figure 1), which exhibits a longitudinal section of the lower end of a tide-water glacier where it pushes out into the sea.

As the sea-cliff of ice recedes and the submerged terrace increases in breadth there comes a time when the buoyancy of the ice at the bottom exceeds its strength, and pieces break off and rise to the surface. The water about the ends of the glaciers is so intensely muddy that the submerged ice-foot is hidden from view, and its presence would not be suspected were it not for the fragments occasionally rising from it. The sudden appearance of these masses of bottom ice at the surface is always startling. While watching the ice-cliffs and admiring the play of colors in the deep crevasses which penetrate them in every direction, or tracing in fancy the strange history of the silent river and wondering in what age the snows fell on the mountains, which are now returning to their parent, the sea, one is frequently awakened by a commotion in the waters below, perhaps several hundred feet in front of the ice-cliffs. At first it seems as if some huge sea-monster had risen from the deep and was lashing the waters into foam; but soon the waters part, and a blue island rises to the surface, carrying hundreds of tons of water, which flows down its sides in cataracts of foam. Some of the bergs turn completely over on emerging, and thus add to the tumult and confusion that attends their birth. The waves roll away in widening circles, to break in surf on the adjacent shores, and an island of ice of the most lovely blue floats serenely away to join the thousands of similar islands that have preceded it. The fragments of the glacier rising from the bottom in this manner are usually larger than those broken from the faces of the ice-cliffs, sometimes measuring 200 or 300 feet, in diameter. Their size and the suddenness with which they rise would insure certain destruction of a vessel venturing too near the treacherous ice-walls.

At the time of our visit to Haenke island, the entire surface of Disenchantment bay and all of Yakutat bay as far southward as we could see formed one vast field of floating ice. Most of the bergs were small, but here and there rose masses which measured 150 by 200 feet on their sides and stood 40 or 50 feet out of the water. The bergs are divided, in reference to color, into three classes—the white, the blue, and the black. The white ones are those that have fallen from the face of the ice-walls or those that have been sufficiently exposed to the atmosphere to become melted at the surface and filled with air cavities. The blue bergs are of many shades and tints, finding their nearest match in color in Antwerp blue. These are the ones that have recently risen from the submerged ice-foot, or have turned over owing to a change of position in the center of gravity. Rapid as is the

VOL. III, 1891   PL. 19

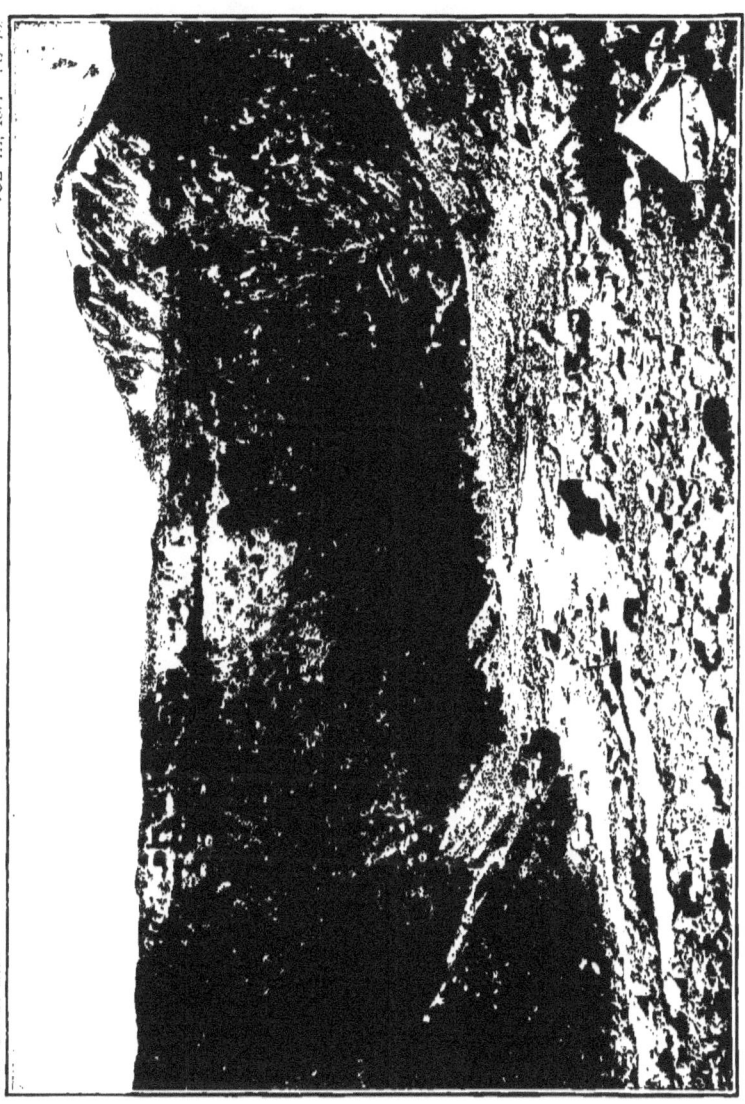

WALL OF ICE ON EASTERN SIDE OF THE ATREVIDA GLACIER

melting of the ice when exposed to the air, it seems to liquefy
even more quickly when submerged. The changes thus produced finally cause the bergs to reverse their positions in the
water. This is done without the slightest warning, and is one of
the greatest dangers to be guarded against while canoeing among
them. The white color presented by the majority of the bergs is
changed to blue when they become stranded, and the surf breaks
over them and dissolves away their porous surfaces. A few of
the bergs are black in color, owing to the dirt and stones that
they carry on their surfaces or frozen in their mass. Quantities
of débris are thus floated away from the tide-water glaciers and
strewn over the bottoms of the adjacent inlets.

This digression may be wearisome, but one cannot stand on
Haenke island without wishing to know all the secrets of the
great ice-streams that flow silently before him.

Returning from our commanding station at the summit of the
island to where we left our canoe, we were surprised and not a
little startled to find that the tide had run out and left the strand
between our canoe and the water completely blocked with huge
fragments of ice. There was no way left for us to launch our
canoe except by cutting away and leveling off the ice with our
axe, so as to form a trail over which we could drag it to the
water. This we did, and then, poising the canoe on a low flat
berg, half of which extended beneath the water, I took my place
in it with paddle in hand, while Christie and Crumback, waiting
for the moment when a large wave rolled in, launched the canoe
far out in the surf. By the vigorous use of my paddle I succeeded in reaching smooth water and brought the canoe close
under the cliff forming the southern side of the cove, where the
men were able to drop in as a wave rolled under us.

We slowly worked our way down the bay through blue lanes
in the ice-pack, against an incoming tide, and reached our tents
near sunset. Thus ended one of the most enjoyable and most
instructive days at Yakutat bay.

From Yakutat Bay to Blossom Island.

Our camp on the shore of Yakutat bay was held for several
days after returning from Haenke island, but in the meantime
an advance-camp was established on the side of the Lucia
glacier, from which Mr. Kerr and myself made explorations
ahead.

Before leaving the base-camp I visited Black glacier for the purpose of taking photographs and studying the appearance of an old glacier far spent and fast passing away. This, like the Galiano glacier, is a good example of a great number of ice-streams in the same region which are covered from side to side with débris. The cañon walls on either side rise precipitously, and their lower slopes, for the height of 200 or 300 feet, are bare of vegetation. The surface of the glacier has evidently sunken to this extent within a period too short to allow of the accumulation of soil and the rooting of plants on the slopes. The banks referred to are in part below the upper limit of timber growth, and the adjacent surfaces are covered with bushes, grasses, and flowers. Under the climatic conditions there prevailing, it is evident that the formation of soil and the spreading of plants over areas abandoned by ice is a matter of comparatively few years. It is for this reason that a very recent retreat of Black glacier is inferred. Many of the glaciers in southern Alaska give similar evidence of recent contraction, and it is evident that a climatic change is in progress which is either decreasing the winter's snow or increasing the summer's heat. The most sensitive indicators of these changes, responding even more quickly than does the vegetation, are the glaciers.

The fourth of July was spent by us in cutting a trail up the steep mountain slope to the amphitheatre visited during my first tramp. No one can appreciate the density and luxuriance of the vegetation on the lower mountain in that region until he has cut a passage through it. Seven men, working continuously for six or seven hours with axes and knives, were able to open a comparatively good trail about a mile in length. The remainder of the way was along stream courses and up bowlder-washes, which were free from vegetation. In the afternoon, having finished our task, a half-holiday was spent in an exciting search for two huge brown bears discovered by one of the party, but they vanished before the guns could be brought out.

The next day an advance-camp was made in the amphitheatre above timber line, and there Mr. Kerr and myself passed the night, molested only by swarms of mosquitoes, and the day following occupied an outstanding butte as a topographical station. In the afternoon of the same day the advance-camp was moved to the border of the Atrevida glacier at a point already described, where a muddy stream gushes out from under the ice.

VIEW ON THE ATREVIDA GLACIER.

Our next advance-camp, established a few days later, was at Terrace point, as we called the extreme end of the mountain spur separating the Lucia and Atrevida glaciers. These ice-streams were formerly much higher than now, and when at their flood formed terraces along the mountain side, which remain distinctly visible to the present day. The space between the two glaciers at the southern end of the mountain spur became filled with bowlders and stones carried down on the side of the ice-streams, and, as the glaciers contracted, added a tapering point to the mountain. Between the present surface of the ice and the highest terrace left at some former time there are many ridges, sloping down stream, which record minor changes in the fluctuation of the ice. A portion of one of these terraces is seen to the left in plate 10.

Terrace point, like all the lower portions of the mountain spurs extending southward from the main range, is densely clothed with vegetation, and during the short summers is a paradise of flowers. Our tent was pitched on a low terrace just beyond the border of the ice. The steep bluff rising to an elevation of some 200 feet on the east of our camp was formed by glacial ice buried beneath an absolutely barren covering of stones and dirt. On the west the ascent was still more precipitous, but the slope from base to summit was one mass of gorgeous flowers.

Kerr and myself made several excursions from the camp at Terrace point, and explored the country ahead to the next mountain spur for the purpose of selecting a site for another advance-camp. In the meantime the men were busy in bringing up supplies.

Our reconnoissance westward took us across the Lucia glacier to the mouth of a deep, transverse gorge in the next mountain spur. The congeries of low peaks and knobs south of this pass we named the *Floral hills*, on account of the luxuriance of the vegetation covering them; and the saddle separating them from the mountains to the north was called *Floral pass*.

In crossing the Lucia glacier we experienced the usual difficulties met with on the débris-covered ice-field of Alaska. The way was exceedingly rough, on account of the ridges and valleys on the ice, and on account of the angular condition of the débris resting upon it. Many of the ridges could not conveniently be climbed, owing to the uncertain footing afforded by the angular stones resting on the slippery slope beneath. Fortunately, the crevasses were mostly filled with stones fallen from the sides, so that the danger from open fissures, which has usually to be guarded against in glacial excursions, was obviated; yet, as is usually the case when crevasses become filled with débris, the melting of the adjacent surfaces had caused them to stand in relief and form ridges of loose stones, which were exceedingly troublesome to the traveler.

Near the western side of the Lucia glacier, between Terrace point and Floral pass, there is a huge rounded dome of sandstone rising boldly out of the ice. This corresponds to the " nunataks " of the Greenland ice-fields, and was covered by ice when the glaciation was more intense than at present. On the northern side of the island the ice is forced high up on its flanks, and is deeply covered with moraines; but on the southwestern side its base is low and skirted by a sand plain deposited in a valley formerly occupied by a lake.. The melting of the glacier has, in fact, progressed so far that the dome of rock is free from ice on its southern side, and is connected with the border of the valley toward the west by the sand plain. This plain is composed of gravel and sand deposited by streams which at times became dammed lower down and expanded into a lake. Sunken areas and holes over portions of the lake bottom show that it rests, in part at least, upon a bed of ice.

The most novel and interesting feature in the Lucia glacier is a glacial river which bursts from beneath a high archway of ice just at the eastern base of the nunatak mentioned above, and flows for about a mile and a half through a channel excavated in the ice, to then enter the mouth of another tunnel and become lost to view. An illustration of this strange river and of the mouth of the tunnel in the débris-covered ice into which it rolls, reproduced from a photograph by a mechanical process, is given on plate 14 (page 110), and another view of the mouth of the same tunnel is presented in the succeeding plate. This is the finest example of a glacial river that it has ever been my good fortune to examine.

The stream is swift, and its waters are brown and heavy with sediment. Its breadth is about 150 feet. For the greater part of its way, where open to sunlight, it flows between banks of ice and over an icy floor. Fragments of its banks, and portions of

ENTRANCE TO AN ICE TUNNEL, FORMERLY THE OUTLET OF A GLACIAL LAKE.

the sides and roof of the tunnel from which it emerges, are swept along by the swift current, or stranded here and there in mid-stream. The sand plain already mentioned borders the river for a portion of its course, and is flooded when the lower tunnel is obstructed.

The archway under which the stream disappears is about fifty feet high, and the tunnel retains its dimensions as far as one can see by looking in at its mouth. Where the stream emerges is unknown; but the emergence could no doubt be discovered by examining the border of the glacier some miles southward. No explorer has yet been bold enough to enter the tunnel and drift through with the stream, although this could possibly be done without great danger. The greatest risk in such an undertaking would be from falling blocks of ice. While I stood near the mouth of the tunnel there came a roar from the dark cavern within, reverberating like the explosion of a heavy blast in the chambers of a mine, that undoubtedly marked the fall of an ice mass from the arched roof. The course of the stream below the mouth of the tunnel may be traced for some distance by scarps in the ice above, formed by the settling of the roof. Some of these may be traced in the illustrations. When the roof of the tunnel collapses so completely as to obstruct the passage, a lake is formed above the tunnel, and when the obstruction is removed the streams draining the glacier are flooded.

At the mouth of the tunnel there are always confused noises and rhythmic vibrations to be heard in the dark recesses within. The air is filled with pulsations like deep organ notes. It takes but little imagination to transform these strange sounds into the voices and songs of the mythical inhabitants of the nether regions.

Toward the right of the tunnel, as shown on plate 14, there appears a portion of the former river bed, now abandoned, owing to the cutting across of a bend in the stream. The floor of this old channel is mostly of clear, white ice, and has a peculiar, hummocky appearance, which indicates the direction of the current that once flowed over it. A portion of the bed is covered with sand and gravel, and along its border are gravel terraces resting on ice. These occurrences illustrate the fact that rivers flowing through channels of ice are governed by the same general laws as the more familiar surface streams.

After examining this glacial river, during our first excursion on the Lucia glacier, we reached its western banks by crossing above the upper archway. Traversing the sand plain to the westward, we came to another stream of nearly equal interest, flowing along the western margin of the glacier, past the end of the deep gorge called Floral pass. A small creek, flowing down the pass, joins the stream and skirts the glacier just below the mouth of a wild gorge on the side of the main valley. This stream once flowed along the border of the Lucia glacier when it was much higher than now, and began the excavation of a channel in the rock, which was retained after the surface of the glacier was lowered by melting. It still flows in a rock-cut channel for about a mile before descending to the border of the glacier as it exists at present. The geologist will see at once that this is a peculiar example of superimposed drainage. The gorge cut by the stream is a deep narrow trench with rough angular cliffs on either side, and is a good example of a water-cut cañon. When the Lucia glacier melts away and leaves the broad-bottomed valley clear of ice, the deep narrow gorge on its western side, running parallel with its longer axes, but a thousand feet or more above its bottom, will remain as one of the evidences of a former ice invasion.

During our reconnoissance we turned back at the margin of the second river, but a day or two later reached the same point with the camp hands and camping outfit, and, placing a rope from bank to bank, effected a crossing. Our next camp was in Floral pass. From there we occupied a topographical station on the summit of the Floral hills, and made another reconnoissance ahead, across the *Hayden glacier*,* to the next mountain spur.

Floral pass, like so many of the topographical features examined during the recent expedition, has a peculiar history. It is a comparatively low-grade gorge leading directly across the end of an angular mountain range forming one of the spurs of Mount Cook. The position of the pass was determined by an east-and-west fault and by the erosion of soft shales turned up on edge along the line of displacement. At its head it is shut in by the Hayden glacier, which flows past it and forms a wall of ice about two hundred feet high. The water flowing out from beneath the side of the glacier forms a muddy creek, which finds its way over a bowlder-covered bed in the bottom of the gorge to the border of Lucia glacier. Along the sides of the gorge there are

* Named in honor of the late Dr. Ferdinand V. Hayden, founder of the United States Geological Survey of the Territories.

DELTAS IN AN ABANDONED LAKE BED.

many terraces, which record a complicated history. Evenly stratified clays near its lower end, adjacent to the Lucia glacier, show that it was at one time occupied in part by a lake. Above the lacustral beds there are water-worn deposits, indicating that at a later date the gorge was filled from side to side by moraines and coarse stream deposits several hundred feet thick. These were excavated, and portions were left clinging to the hill-sides, forming the terraces of to-day. Diverse slopes in the terraces suggest that the drainage may at times have been reversed, according as the Lucia or the Hayden glacier was the higher.

The routes between our various camps, scattered along between Yakutat bay and Blossom island, were traversed several times by every member of the party. To traverse the same trail several times with heavy loads, and perhaps in rain and mist, is disheartening work which I will spare the reader the effort of following even in fancy.

From our camp in Floral pass another reconnoissance ahead was made by Mr. Kerr and myself, as already mentioned. These advances, each one of which told us something new, were the most interesting portions of our journey. The little adventures and experiences of each advance were reported and talked over when we rejoined our companions around the camp-fire at night, and were received with gratifying interest by the men.

A view of the Hayden glacier from the Floral hills showed us that it differed from any of the glaciers previously traversed. Its surface, where we planned to cross it, was free of débris except along the margins and also near the center, where we could distinguish a light medial moraine. Farther southward, near the terminus of the glacier, its surface from side to side was buried beneath a sheet of stones and dirt. As in many other instances, the débris on the lower portion of the glacier has been concentrated at the surface, owing to the melting of the ice, so as to form a continuous sheet.

Early one morning, while traveling over the torrent-swept bowlders in the stream-bed on our way up Floral pass, we were a little startled at seeing the head of a bear just visible through the flowers fringing the bank. Before a shot could be fired, he vanished, and remained perfectly quiet among the bushes for several minutes. But a trembling of the branches at length betrayed his presence, and a few minutes later he came out in full view, his yellow-brown coat giving him the appearance of a huge dog. Standing on a rounded mound he looked inquiringly down the valley, with his shaggy side in full view. I fired—but missed my aim. The unsuccessful hunter always has an excuse for his failure: I had never before used the rifle I carried, and the hair-trigger with which it was provided deceived me. Fortunately for the bear, and probably still more fortunately for me, the bullet went far above the mark. The huge beast vanished again, although the vegetation was not dense, and left us wondering how such a large animal could disappear so quickly and so completely in such an open region. On searching for his tracks, we found that he had traversed for a few rods the plant-covered terrace on which he was first discovered, and then escaped up a lateral gorge to a broader terrace above.

Reaching the head of the Floral pass and climbing the hill of débris bordering the Hayden glacier, we came out upon the clear, white ice of the central portion of the ice-stream. The ice was greatly crevassed, but nearly all the gaps in its surface could be crossed by jumping or else by ice-bridges. The most interesting feature presented by the glacier was the way in which it yields itself to the inequality of the rocks over which it flows. Starting on the eastern side, below the entrance to Floral pass, and extending northwestward diagonally across the stream, there is a line of steep descent in the rocks beneath, which causes the ice to be greatly broken. This is not properly an ice-fall, except near the confining walls of the cañon; but it might be called an ice-rapid. The ice bends down over the subglacial scarp with many long breaks, but does not form pinnacles, as in many similar instances where the descent is greater, and true ice cascades occur. The most practicable way for crossing the glacier was to ascend the stream above the line of rapids for some distance, and then follow diagonally down its center, finally veering westward to the opposite bank. By following this course, and making a double curve like the letter S, we could cross the steep descent in the center, where it was least crevassed.

The marginal moraines on the Hayden glacier are formed of fragments of brown and gray sandstone and black shale of all sizes and shapes. It is clear that this débris was gathered by the cliffs bordering the glacier on either side. The medial moraine which first appears at the surface just above the rapids is of a different character, and tells that the higher peaks of Mount Cook are composed, in part at least, of a different material from

A RIVER ON THE LUCIA GLACIER.

the spurs projecting from it. The medial moraine looks black from a distance, but, on traversing it, it was found to be composed mainly of dark-green gabbro and serpentine. The débris is scattered over the surface in a belt several rods wide; but it is not deep, as the ice can almost everywhere be seen between the stones. Where the fragments of rock are most widely separated, there are fine illustrations of the manner in which small, dark stones absorb the heat of the sun and melt the ice beneath more rapidly than the surrounding surface, sinking into the ice so as to form little wells, several inches deep, filled with clear water. Larger stones, which are not warmed through during a day's sunshine, protect the ice beneath while the adjacent surface is melted, and consequently become elevated on pillars or pedestals of ice. The stones thus elevated are frequently large, and form tables which are nearly always inclined southward. In other instances the ice over large areas, especially along the center of the medial moraine, was covered with cones of fine, angular fragments from a few inches to three or four feet in height. These were not really piles of gravel, as they seemed, but consisted of cones of ice, sheeted over with thin layers of small stones. The secret of their formation, long since discovered on the glaciers of Switzerland, is that the gravel is first concentrated in a hole in the ice and, as the general surface melts away, acts like a large stone and protects the ice beneath. It is raised on a pedestal, but the gravel at the borders continually rolls down the sides and a conical form is the result.

Where we crossed the Hayden glacier it is only about a mile broad in a direct line; but to traverse it by the circuitous route rendered necessary by the character of its surface required about three hours of hard tramping, even when unincumbered with packs. From the center of the glacier a magnificent view may be obtained of the snow-covered domes of Mount Cook, from which rugged mountain ridges stretch southward like great arms and enclose the white snow-field from which the glacier flows. At an elevation of 2,500 feet the icy portion disappears beneath the névé on which not a trace of débris is visible. All the higher portions of the mountains are white as snow can make them, except where the pinnacles and precipices are too steep to retain a covering.

On reaching the western side of the glacier we found a bare space on the bordering cliffs, about a hundred feet high, which has been abandoned by the ice so recently that it is not yet grassed over. Above this came the luxuriant and beautiful vegetation covering all the lower mountain slopes.

The mountain spur just west of the glacier, like several of the ridges stretching southward from the higher mountains, ends in a group of hills somewhat separate from the main ridge. The hills are covered with a rank vegetation, and in places support a dense growth of spruce trees. Reaching the grassy summit, we had a fine, far-reaching view of the unexplored region toward the west, and of the vast plateau of ice stretching southward beyond the reach of the vision. West of our station, another great ice-stream, named the *Marvine glacier*, in honor of the late A. R. Marvine, flows southward with a breadth exceeding that of any of the icy streams yet crossed. Beyond the Marvine glacier, and forming its western border, there is an exceedingly rugged mountain range trending northeast and southwest. Although this is, topographically, a portion of the mountain mass forming Mount Cook, its prominence and its peculiar geological structure render it important that it should have an independent name. In acknowledgment of the services to science rendered by the first state geologist of Massachusetts, it is designated the *Hitchcock range* on our maps. Rising above the angular crest line of this mountain mass towers the pyramidal summit of Mount St. Elias, seemingly as distant as when we first beheld it from near Yakutat bay.

About a mile west of the hill on which we stood, and beyond the bed of a lake now drained of its waters by a tunnel leading southward through the ice, rose a steep, rocky island out of the glaciers, its summit overgrown with vegetation and dark with spruce trees. This oasis in a sea of ice, subsequently named Blossom island, we chose as the most favorable site for our next advance-camp.

We then returned to our camp in Floral pass, and a day or two later Kerr and Christie started on a side trip up the Hayden glacier, to be absent five days. During this trip the weather was stormy, and only allowed half an hour for topographical work when a somewhat favorable station was reached. This was of great service, however, in mapping the country, as it gave a station of considerable elevation on the side of Mount Cook. The trip was nearly all above the snow-line, and was relieved by many novel experiences.

ENTRANCE TO A GLACIAL TUNNEL.

While Kerr and Christie were away, I assisted the camp hands in advancing to Blossom island. Our first day's work consisted in packing loads across the Hayden glacier to the wooded hills on its western border, reached during the reconnoissance described above. The weather was stormy, and a dense fog rolled in from the ocean, obscuring the mountains, and compelling us to find our way across the glacier as best we could without landmarks. Patiently threading our way among crevasses, we at length came in sight of the forests on the extremity of the mountain spur toward the west, and concluded to camp there until the weather was more favorable. We climbed the bare slope bordering the glacier, and forced our way through the dripping vegetation to an open space beside a little stream and near some aged spruce trees that would furnish good fuel for a camp-fire. We were glad of a refuge, but did not fully appreciate the fact that our tents were in a paradise of flowers until the next morning, when the sun shone clear and bright for a few hours. We hailed with delight the world of summer beauty with which we were surrounded. Our camp was in a little valley amid irregular hills of débris left by the former ice invasion, each of which was a rounded dome of flowers. The desolate ice-fields were completely shut out from view by the rank vegetation. On the slope above us, dark spruce trees loaded with streamers of moss, and seemingly many centuries old, formed a background for the floral decoration with which the ground was everywhere covered. Flowering plants and ferns were massed in such dense luxuriance that the streams were lost in gorgeous banks of bloom.

Reluctantly we returned to Floral pass for another load of camp supplies, and late in the afternoon pressed on to Blossom island, where we again pitched our tents in rain and mist, and again, when the storm cleared away, found ourselves in an untrodden paradise. Kerr and Christie rejoined us at Blossom island on July 31, and we were once more ready for an advance.

BLOSSOM ISLAND.

Our camp on Blossom island was near a small pond of water and close beside a thick grove of spruce trees on the western side of the land-mass. The tents were so placed as to secure an unobstructed view to the westward; and they were visible, in turn, to parties descending from the mountains toward the northwest, whither our work soon led us.

The sides of Blossom island are rough and precipitous. The glaciers flowing past it cut away the rocks and, as the surface of the ice-fields was lowered, left them in many places in rugged cliffs bare of vegetation. The top of the island was also formerly glaciated and in part covered with débris; but the ice retreated so long ago that the once desolate surface has become clothed in verdure. Everywhere there are dense growths of flowers, ferns and berry bushes. On the rocky spurs, thrifty spruce trees, festooned with drooping streamers, shelter luxuriant banks of mosses, lichens and ferns. There was no evidence that human hand had ever plucked a flower in that luxuriant garden; not a trace could be found of man's previous invasion. The only trails were those left by the bears in forcing their way through the dense vegetation in quest of succulent roots. Later in the season, when the berries ripened, there was a feast spread invitingly for all who chose to partake. On the warm summer days the air was filled with the perfume of the flowers, birds flitted in and out of the shady grove, and insects hummed in the glad sunlight; the freshness and beauty on every hand made this island seem a little Eden, preserved with all its freshness and fragrance from the destroying hand of man.

This oasis in a desert of ice is so beautiful and displays so many instructive and attractive features that I wish the reader to come with me up the flowery slopes and study the interesting pictures to be seen from its summit.

The narrow ravine back of our camp is festooned and overhung with tall ferns, shooting out from the thickets on either hand like bending plumes. You will notice at a glance, if perchance your youthful excursions happened to be in the northeastern states, as were mine, that many of the plants about us are old friends, or at least former acquaintances. The tall fern nodding so gracefully as we pass is an *Asplenium*, but of ranker growth than in most southern regions. These tall white flowers with aspiring, flat-topped umbles, looking like rank caraway plants, but larger and more showy, belong to the genus *Archangelica*, and are at home in the Cascade range and the Rocky Mountains as well as here. The lily-like plant growing so profusely, especially in the moist dells, with tall, slim spikes of greenish flowers and long parallel veined leaves, is *Veratrum viride*. These brilliant yellow monkey-flowers, bending so gracefully over the banks of the pond, are closely related to the little

MALASPINA GLACIER, FROM BLOSSOM ISLAND.

Mimulus which nods to its own golden reflection in many of the
brooks of New England. That purple *Epilobium*, with now and
then a pure white variety, so common everywhere on these hills,
is the same wanderer that we have seen over many square miles
beneath the burnt woods of Maine. These bushes with obscure
white flowers, looking like little waxen bells, we recognize at
once as huckleberries; in a short time they will be loaded with
luscious fruit. Inviting couches of moss beneath the spruce
trees are festooned and decorated with fairy shapes of brown and
green, that recall many a long ramble among the Adirondack
hills and in the Canadian woods. The lycopods, equiseta and
ferns are many of them identical with the tracery on mossy
mounds covering fallen hemlocks in the Otsego woods in New
York, but display greater luxuriance and fresher and more brilliant colors. That graceful little beach-fern, here and there faded
to a rich brown, foretelling of future changes, is identical with
the little fairy form we used to gather long ago along the borders
of the Great Lakes. Asters and gentians, delicate orchids and
purple lupines, besides many less familiar plants, crowd the hill-
sides and deck the unkempt meadows with a brilliant mass of
varied light. In the full sunshine, the hill-slopes appear as if
the fields of petals clothing them had the prism's power, and
were spreading a web of rainbow tints over the lush leaves and
grasses below.

On our return to Blossom island, late in September, we found
many of the flowers faded, but in their places there was a profusion of berries nearly as brilliant in color as the petals that
heralded their coming. Many of the thickets, inconspicuous
before, had then a deep, rich yellow tint, due to an abundance
of luscious salmon berries, larger than our largest blackberries.
The huckleberries were also ripe, and in wonderful profusion.
These additions to our table were especially appreciated after
living for more than a month in the snow. The ash trees were
holding aloft great bunches of scarlet berries, even deeper and
richer in color than the ripe leaves on the same brilliant branches.
The deep woods were brilliant with the broad yellow leaves of
the Devil's club, above which rose spikes of crimson berries.
The dense thickets of currant bushes, so luxuriant that it was
difficult to force one's way through them, had received a dusky,
smoke-like tint, due to abundant blue-black strings of fruit suspended all along the under sides of the branches.

Let us not look too far ahead, however. Wandering on over the sunny slopes, where the gardener has forgotten to separate the colors or to divide the flower banks, we gain the top of the island; but so dense are the plants about us, and so eager is each painted cup to expand freely in the sunlight at the expense of its neighbors, that we have to beat them down with our alpenstocks—much as we dislike to mar the beauty of the place—before we can recline on the thick turf beneath and study the strange landscape before us.

The foreground of every view is a bank of flowers nodding and swaying in the wind, but all beyond is a frozen desert. The ice-fields before us, with their dark bands of débris, are a picture of desolation. The creative breath has touched only the garden which we, the first of wanderers, have invaded. The land before us is entirely without human associations. No battles have there been fought, no kings have ruled, no poets have sung of its ruggedness, and no philosopher has explained its secrets. Yet it has its history, its poetry, and its philosophy!

The mountains toward the north are too near at hand to reveal their grandeur; only the borders of the vast snow-fields covering all of these upper slopes are in view. In the deep cañon with perpendicular walls, just north of our station, but curving westward so that its upper course is concealed from view, there flows a secondary glacier which forces its terminal moraine high up on the northern slope of Blossom island, but does not now join the ice-field on the south. Streams of turbid water flow from this glacier on each side of the oasis on which we stand and unite at the mouth of a dark tunnel in the ice toward the south.

The barren gravel plain just east of our station, and at the foot of the glacier from the north, is the bed of a glacial lake which has been drained through the tunnel in the ice. On our way to Blossom island we crossed this area and found that it had but recently lost its waters. Miniature terraces on the gravel banks forming the sides of the basin marked the height to which the waters last rose, and all the slopes formerly submerged were covered with a thin layer of sediment. On the sides of the basin where this fresh lining rests on steep slopes there are beautiful frettings made by rills in the soft sediment. The stream from the glacier now meanders across this sand plain, dividing as it goes into many branches, which unite on approach-

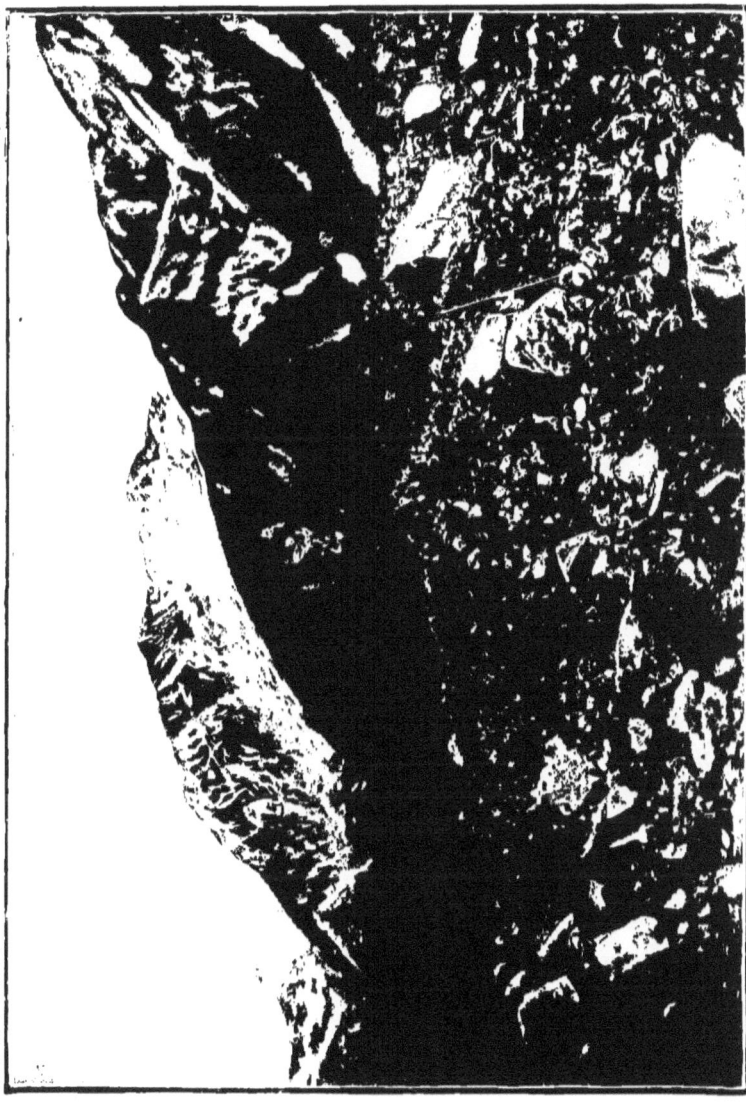

MORAINES ON THE MARVIN GLACIER.

ing the dark archway below. The lake is extremely irregular in its behavior, and may be filled and emptied several times in a season. The waters are either restrained or flow freely, according as the tunnel through which they discharge is obstructed or open. The lake is typical of a class. Similar basins may be found about many of the spurs projecting into the Malaspina glacier.

A little west of the glacier to which I have directed your attention there is a narrow mountain gorge occupied by another glacier, of small size but having all the principal characteristics of even the largest Alpine glaciers of the region. It is less than half a mile in length, has a high grade, and is fed by several lateral branches. Its surface is divided into an ice region below and a névé region above. It has lateral and medial moraines, ice pinnacles, crevasses, and many other details peculiar to glaciers. From its extremity, which is dark with dirt and stones, there flows a stream of turbid water. It is, in fact, a miniature similitude of the ice-streams on the neighboring mountain, some of which are forty or fifty miles in length and many times wider in their narrowest part than the little glacier before us is long. The more thoroughly we become acquainted with the mountains of southern Alaska the more interesting and more numerous do the Alpine glaciers of the third order become. Already, thousands could be enumerated.

I will not detain my imaginary companion longer with local details, but turn at once to the objects which will ever be the center of attraction to visitors who may chance to reach this remote island in the ice. Looking far up the Marvine glacier, beyond the tapering pinnacles and rugged peaks about its head, you will see spires and cathedral-like forms of the purest white projected against the northern sky. They recall at once the ecclesiastic architecture of the Old World; but instead of being dim and faded by time they seem built of immaculate marble. They have a grandeur and repose seen only in mountains of the first magnitude. The cathedral to the right, with the long roof-like crest and a tapering spire at its eastern terminus, is Mount Augusta: its elevation is over 13,000 feet. A little to the west, and equally beautiful but slightly less in elevation, is Mount Malaspina—a worthy monument to the unfortunate navigator whose name it bears. These peaks are on the main St. Elias range, but from our present point of view they form only the

background of a magnificent picture. Later in the season our
tents were pitched at their very bases, and they then revealed
their full grandeur and fulfilled every promise given by distant
views.

The rugged Hitchcock range bordering the distant margin of
the Marvine glacier, like the mountains near at hand and the
rocky island on which we stand, is composed of sandstone and
shale, but presents one interesting feature, to which I shall direct
your attention. The trend of the range is northeast and southwest, but the strata of which it is composed run east and west
and are inclined northward. As the range is some eight miles
long, these conditions would seem to indicate a thickness of many
thousands of feet for the rocks of which it is composed; yet the
beds were deposited in horizontal sheets of sand and mud of
very late date, as will be shown farther on. But the great
apparent thickness of the strata is deceptive; a nearer examination would reveal the fact that the rocks have been so greatly
crushed that even a hand specimen can scarcely be broken off
with fresh surfaces. More than this, the black shale, exhibiting
the greatest amount of crushing, is usually in wedge-shaped
masses, which, in some cases at least, are bordered by what are
known as thrust planes, nearly coinciding with the bedding
planes of the strata. The rocks have been fractured and crushed
together in such a way as to pile fragments of the same layer on
top of each other, and thus to increase greatly their apparent
thickness. In the elevations before us the thrust planes are
tipped northeastwardly, and it would seem that the force that
produced them acted from that direction. The apparent thickness of the beds has thus been increased many times. What
their original thickness was, it is not now possible to say. Similar
indications of a lateral crushing in the rocks may be found in
several of the mountain spurs between the Hitchcock range and
Yakutat bay; but space will not permit me to follow this sub-
ject further.

Turning from the mountains, we direct our eyes seaward; but
it is a sea of ice that meets our view and not the blue Pacific.
Far as the eye can reach toward the west, toward the south, and
toward the southeast there is nothing in view but a vast plateau
of ice or barren débris fields resting on ice and concealing it from
view. This is the Malaspina glacier.

On the border of the ice, just below the cliffs on which we

HITCHCOCK RANGE, FROM NEAR DOME PASS.

stand, there is a belt of débris perhaps five miles in breadth,
which almost completely conceals the ice beneath. Portions of
this moraine are covered by vegetation, and in places it is brill-

FIGURE 2—*View of a glacial Lakelet (drawn from a Photograph).*

iant with flowers. The vegetation is most abundant on the
nearer border and fades away toward the center of the glacier.
Its distant border, adjacent to the white ice-field beyond, is

absolutely bare and desolate. An attempt has been made to re-produce this scene in the picture forming plate 16. The drawing is from a photograph and shows the barren débris field stretch-ing away towards the southwest. The extreme southern end of the Hitchcock range appears at the right. In the distance is the white ice of the central part of the Malaspina glacier. Far be-yond, faintly outlined against the sky, are the snow-covered hills west of Icy bay. The flowers in the foreground are growing on the crest of the steep bluff bordering Blossom island on the south.

On the moraine-covered portion, especially where plants have taken root, there are hundreds, perhaps thousands, of lakelets occupying kettle-shaped depressions. A view of one of these interesting reservoirs in the ice is given in figure 2. If we should go down to the glacier and examine such a lakelet near at hand, we should find that the cliffs of ice surrounding them are usually unsymmetrical, being especially steep and rugged on one side

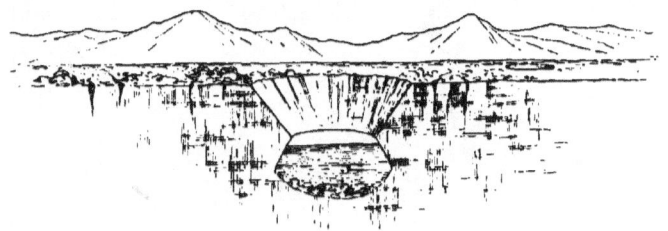

FIGURE 3—Section of a glacial lakelet.

and low or perhaps wanting entirely on the other. But there is no regularity in this respect; the steep slopes may face in any direction. On bright days the encircling walls are always drip-ping with water produced by the melting of the ice; little rills are constantly flowing down their sides and plunging in minia-ture cataracts into the lake below; the stones at the top of the ice-cliffs, belonging to the general sheet of débris covering the glacier, are continually being undermined and precipitated into the water. A curious fact in reference to the walls of the lakelets is that the melting of the ice below the surface is more rapid than above, where it is exposed to the direct rays of the sun. As a result the depressions have the form of an hour-glass, as indicated in the accompanying section.

Beyond the bordering moraines at our feet, we can look far out over the ice-plateau and view hundreds of square miles of its

frozen surface. At the same time we obtain glimpses of other
vast ice-fields toward the west, beyond Icy bay; but their limits
in that direction are unknown.

Later in the season I made an excursion far out on the Malaspina glacier from the extreme southern end of the Hitchcock
range, and became acquainted with many of its peculiarities. Its
surface, instead of being a smooth snow-field, as it appears from
a distance, is roughened by thousands of crevasses, many of
which are filled with clear, blue water. Over hundreds of square
miles the surface appears as if a giant plow had passed over it,
leaving the ice furrowed with crevasses. The crevasses are not
broad; usually one can cross them at a bound. They appear to
be the scars left by rents in the tributary ice-streams.

The stillness far out on the great ice-field is immediately
noticed by one who has recently traversed the sloping surfaces
of the tributary glaciers. It is always silent on that vast frozen
plateau. There are no surface streams and no lakes; not a rill
murmurs along its channel of ice; no cascades are formed by
streams plunging into moulins and crevasses. The water produced by the melting of the ice finds its way down into the
glacier and perhaps to its bottom, and must there form rivers of
large size; but no indications of their existence can be obtained
at the surface. The icy surface is undulating, and resembles in
some respects the great rolling prairies of the west; it is a prairie
of ice. In the central portion not a shoot of vegetation casts its
shadow, and scarcely a fragment of rock can be found. The
boundaries of the vast plateau have never been surveyed, but its
area cannot be less than five hundred square miles. The clear
ice of the center greatly exceeds the extent of the moraine-covered borders. It has a general elevation of fifteen or sixteen
hundred feet, being highest near the end of the Hitchcock range,
where the Seward glacier comes in, and decreasing from there in
all directions. From the summit of Blossom island and other
commanding stations it is evident that the dark moraine belts
about its borders are compound and record a varied history.
Far away toward the southeast the individual elements may be
distinguished. The dark bands of débris sweep around in great
curves and concentric, swirl-like figures, which indicate that there
are complicated currents in the seemingly motionless plateau.

The Malaspina glacier belongs to a class of ice bodies not previously recognized, which are formed at the bases of mountains by the union of several glaciers from above. Their position suggests the name of *Piedmont glaciers* for the type. They differ from continental glaciers in the fact that they are formed by the union of ice-streams and are not the sources from which ice-streams flow. The supply from the tributary glacier is counterbalanced by melting and evaporation.

If the reader has become interested in the vast ice-fields about Blossom island, he may wish to continue our acquaintance and go with me into the great snow-fields on the higher mountains, where the ice-rivers feeding the Malaspina glacier have their sources.

Life Above the Snow-Line.

Early on the morning of August 2, all necessary preparations having been made the day previous, we started in the direction of the great snow peak to be seen at the head of the Marvine glacier, where we hoped to find a pass leading through the mountains which would enable us to reach the foot of Mount St. Elias or to discover a practicable way across the main range into the unknown country toward the north.

All of the camp hands were with us at the start, except Stamy and White, who had been despatched to Port Mulgrave to purchase shoes. All but Crumback and Lindsley were to return to Blossom island, however, after leaving their loads at a rendezvous as far from Blossom island as could be reached in a day and allow sufficient time to return to the base-camp. Kerr and myself, with the two camp hands mentioned, were to press on to the snow-fields above. We took with us a tent, blankets, rations, an oil-stove, and a supply of coal oil, and felt equal to any emergency that might arise.

The morning of our departure was thick and foggy, with occasional showers, and the weather grew worse instead of better as we advanced. All the mountains were soon shut out from view by the vast vapor banks that settled down from above, and we had little except the general character of the glacier to guide us.

Our way at first led up the eastern border of the Marvine glacier, over seemingly interminable fields of angular débris. Traveling on the rugged moraine, some idea of which may be obtained from plate 17, was not only tiresome in the extreme, but ruinous to boots and shoes. On passing the mouth of the first lateral gorge (about a mile from Blossom island), from which flows a secondary glacier, we could look up the bed of the steep ravine to the white precipices beyond, which seemed to descend out of the clouds, and were scarred by avalanches; but all of the higher peaks were shrouded from view. At noon we passed the mouth of a second and larger gorge, which discharges an important tributary. We then left the border of the glacier and traveled up its center, the crevasses at the embouchures of the tributary stream being too numerous and too wide to be crossed without great difficulty.

In the center of the Marvine glacier there is a dark medial moraine, composed mainly of débris of gabbro and serpentine, of the same character as the medial moraine on the Hayden glacier, already briefly mentioned. Here, too, we found broad areas covered with sand cones and glacial tables. There are also rushing streams, flowing in channels of ice, which finally plunge into crevasses or in well-like moulins and send back a deep roar from the caverns beneath. The murmurs of running waters, heard on every hand, seem to indicate that the whole glacier is doomed to melt away in a single season.

Early in the afternoon we reached the junction of the two main branches of the Marvine glacier, and chose the most westerly. We were still traveling over hard blue ice in which the blue and white vein-structure characteristic of glaciers could be plainly distinguished. The borders of the ice-streams were dark with lateral moraines; but after passing the last great tributary coming in from the northeast we reached the upper limit of the glacier proper and came to the lower border of the névé fields, above which there is little surface débris. The glacier there flows over a rugged descent, and is greatly broken by its fall. At first we endeavored to find a passage up the center of the crevassed and pinnacled ice, but soon came to an impassable gulf. Turning toward the right, we traversed a ridge of ice between profound gorges and reached the base of the mountain slope bordering the glacier on the east. Our party was now divided: Christie and his companion were left searching for a convenient place to leave the cans of rations they carried, while we, who were to explore the regions above, were endeavoring to find a way up the ice-fall. A shout from our companions below called our attention to the fact that they were unable to reach the border of the glacier, where they had been directed to leave their packs, and that they had left them on the open ice. They waved us "good-bye" and started back toward Blossom island, leaving our little band of four to make the advance.

Descending into a deep black gorge at the border of the ice, formed by its melting back from the bordering cliffs, we clambered upward beneath overhanging ice-walls, from which stones and fragments of ice were occasionally dropping, and finally reached a great snow-bank on the border of the glacier. As the storm still continued, and was even increasing in force, we concluded to find a camping ground soon as possible and make ourselves comfortable as the circumstances would permit.

First Camp in the Snow.

We had now reached the lower limit of perpetual snow. There were no more moraines on the surface of the glacier, and no bare rock surfaces large enough to hold a tent. The entire region was snow-mantled as far as the eye could see, except where pinnacles and cliffs too steep and rugged for the snow to accumulate rose above the general surface. A little to one side of the mouth of a steep lateral gorge we found a spot in which a mass of partly disintegrated shale had fallen down from the cliff. We scraped the fragments aside, smoothed the snow beneath, and built a wall of rock along the lower margin. The space above was filled in with fragments of shale, so as to form a shelf on which to pitch our tent. Soon our blankets were spread, with our water-proof coats for a substratum, and supper was prepared over the oil-stove.

Darkness settled down over the mountains, and the storm increased as the night came on. What is unusual in Alaska, the rain fell in torrents, as in the tropics. Our little tent of light cotton cloth afforded great protection, but the rain-drops beat on it with such force that the spray was driven through and made a fine rain within. Weary with many hours of hard traveling over moraines and across crevassed ice, and in an atmosphere saturated with moisture, we rolled ourselves in our blankets, determined to rest in spite of the storm that raged about.

As the rain became heavier, the avalanches, already alarmingly numerous, became more and more frequent: A crash like thunder, followed by the clatter of falling stones, told that many tons of ice and rocks on the mountains to the westward had slid down upon the borders of the glacier; another roar near at hand, caused by an avalanche on our own side of the glacier, was followed by another, another, and still another out in the darkness, no one could tell where. The wilder the storm, the louder and more frequent became the thunder of the avalanches. It seemed as if pandemonium reigned on the mountains. One might fancy that the evil spirits of the hills had prepared for us a reception of their own liking—but decidedly not to the taste of their visitors. Soon there was a clatter and whiz of stones at our door. Looking out I saw rocks as large as one's head bounding past within a few feet of our tent. The stones on the mountain side above had been loosened by the rain, and it was evident that our perch was no longer tenable. Before we could remove our frail shelter to a place of greater safety, a falling rock struck the alpenstock to which the ridge-rope of our tent was fastened and carried it away. Our tent "went by the board," as a sailor would say, and we were left exposed to the pouring rain. Before we could gather up our blankets they were not only soaked, but a bushel or more of mud and stones from the bank above, previously held back by the tent, flowed in upon them. Rolling up our blankets and "caching" the rations, instruments, etc., under a rubber cloth held down by rocks, we hastily dragged our tent-cloth down to the border of the glacier, at the extremity of a tapering ridge, along which it seemed impossible for stones from above to travel. We there pitched our tent on the hard snow, without the luxury of even a few handfuls of shale beneath our blankets. Wet and cold, we sought to wear the night away as best we could, sleep being impossible. Crumback, who had been especially energetic in removing the tent, regardless of his own exposure, was wet and became cold and silent. The oil-stove and a few rations were brought from the cache at the abandoned camp, and soon a dish of coffee was steaming and filling the tent with its delicious odor. Our shelter became comfortably warm and the hot coffee, acting as a stimulant, restored our sluggish circulation. We passed an uncomfortable night and watched anxiously for the dawn. Toward morning a cold wind swept down the glacier and the rain ceased. With the dawn there came indications that the storm had passed, although we were still enveloped in dense clouds and could not decide whether or not a favorable change in the weather had occurred. We were still cold and wet and the desire to return to Blossom island, where all was sunshine and summer, was great. Uncertain as to what would be the wisest course, we packed our blankets and started slowly down the mountain, looking anxiously for signs that the storm had really passed.

An hour after sunrise a rift in the mist above us revealed the wonderful blue of the heavens, and allowed a flood of sunlight to pour down upon the white fields beneath. Never was the August sun more welcome. The mists vanished before its magic touch, leaving here and there fleecy vapor-wreaths festooned along the mountain side; as the clouds disappeared, peak after peak came into view, and snow-domes and glaciers, never seen before, one by one revealed themselves to our astonished eyes. When the curtain was lifted we found ourselves in a new world, more wild and rugged than any we had yet beheld. There was not a tree in sight, and nothing to suggest green fields or flowery hill-sides, except on a few of the lower mountain spurs, where brilliant Alpine blossoms added a touch of color to the pale landscape. All else was stern, silent, motionless winter.

The glacier, clear and white, without a rock on its broken surface, looked from a little distance like a vast snow-covered meadow. We were about a mile above the lower limit of the snow-fields, where the blue ice of the glacier comes out from beneath the névé. The blue ice was deeply buried, and could only be seen in the deepest crevasses. Across the glacier rose the angular cliffs and tapering spires of the Hitchcock range. Every ravine and gulch in its rugged sides was occupied by glaciers, many of which were so broken and crevassed that they looked like frozen cataracts.

Cheered by the bright skies and sun-warmed air, we pushed on up the glacier, taking the center of the stream in order to avoid the crevasses, which were most numerous along its borders. Two or three miles above our first camp we found a place where a thin layer of broken shale covered the snow, at a sufficient distance from the steep slopes above to be out of the reach of avalanches. We there established our second camp after leaving Blossom island, dried our blankets, and spent the remainder of the day basking in the sunlight and gathering energy for coming emergencies.

We found the névé of the Marvine glacier differing greatly from the lower or icy portion previously traversed. Instead of ice with blue and white bands, as is common lower down, the entire surface, and as far down in the crevasses as the eye could distinguish, was composed of compact snow, or snow changed to icy particles resembling hail and having in reality but few of the properties of ordinary snow: it might properly be called névé ice. Usually the thickness of the layers varied from ten to fifteen feet. Separating them were dark lines formed by dust blown over the surface of the glacier and buried by subsequent snow-storms, or by thin blue lines formed by the edges of sheets of ice and showing that the snow surface had been melted during bright sunny days and frozen again at night. The horizontal stratification so plainly marked in all the crevasses in the névé was almost entirely wanting, or at least was not conspicuous, in the lower portion of the glacier, where, instead, we found those narrow blue and white bands already mentioned, the origin of which has been so well described and explained by Tyndall.

The center of the Marvine glacier, as in most similar ice-streams, is higher and less broken by crevasses than its borders. The crevasses at the side trend up stream, as is the case with marginal crevasses generally. In the present instance the courses of these rents could be plainly distinguished on each border of the glacier, when looking down upon it from neighboring slopes. The crevasses occur at quite regular intervals of approximately fifty feet, and diverge from the bank at angles of about 40°. In the banks of snow bordering the glacier similar crevasses diverge from the margin of the flowing glacier and trend down along its banks. The marginal crevasses and the crevasses in the bordering snow-fields, to which no special name has been given, fall nearly in line; but between the two there is a series of irregular cracks and broken snow, sharply defining the border of the moving névé.

The origin of the marginal crevasses trending up stream was explained during the study of the glaciers of Switzerland. The following diagram and explanation illustrating their development are copied from Tyndall:

"Let *A C* be one side of the glacier and *B D* the other; and let the direction of motion be that indicated by the arrow. Let *S T* be a transverse slice of the glacier, taken straight across it, say to-day. A few days or weeks hence the slice will have been carried down, and because the center moves more quickly than the sides it will not remain straight, but will bend into the form *S′ T′*. Supposing *T i* to be a small square of the original slice near the side of the glacier; in the new position the square will be distorted to the lozenge-shaped figure *T′ i′*. Fix your attention upon the diagonal *T i* of the square; in the lower position this diagonal, *if the ice could stretch*, would be lengthened to *T' i'*. But the ice does not stretch; it breaks, and we have a crevasse formed at right angles to *T' i'*. The mere inspection of the diagram will assure you that the crevasse will point obliquely *upward*." *

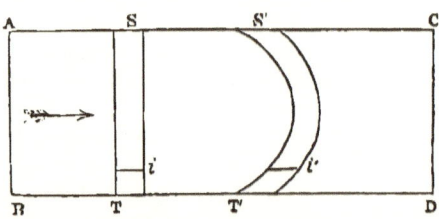

Figure 4—*Diagram illustrating the Formation of marginal Crevasses.*

The explanation given above applies especially to the lower or icy portion of a glacier; above the snow-line other facts appear. When a glacier flows through fields of snow on a level with its surface, crevasses are formed in the adjacent banks. These trend down stream for the same reason that the crevasses in the glacier proper trend up stream—that is, the friction of the moving stream against its banks tends to carry them along, while the portions at a distance are stationary. Fissures are thus opened which trend in the direction in which the glacier moves. The angle made by these crevasses with the axis of the glacier is about the same as those of the marginal crevasses, but in an opposite direction. They are widest near the margin of the glacier and taper to a sharp end towards the stationary snow-banks above. The crevasses in the two series thus fall nearly in line, but are separated by a narrow band of irregularly broken snow, marking the actual border of the glacier. †

After leaving Blossom island the party was divided, and we began a new series of numbers for our camps above the snow-line, although in this narrative and on the accompanying map a single series of numbers for all the camps will be used. While in the field the camps in the snow were usually termed, facetiously, "sardine camps," in allusion to the uncomfortable manner in which we were packed in our tent at night.

* The Forms of Water: International Scientific Series, New York, 1875, pp. 107–108.

† Crevasses in snow-fields through which ice-streams flow will be mentioned again in describing the Seward glacier.

The morning after reaching Camp 12 dawned gloriously bright. The night had been cold, and a heavy frost had silenced every rill from the snow-slopes above. The clear, bracing air gave us renewed energy and a firmer desire to press on. Mr. Kerr and myself made an excursion ahead, while Lindsey and Crumback brought up a load of supplies from the cache left on the glacier below Camp 11.

On gaining the center of the Marvine glacier we had a magnificent view down the broad ice-stream, bordered on either hand by towering, snow-laden precipices, and changing, as the eye followed the downward slope, from pure white to brown and black in the distance. Far below we could barely discern the wooded summit of Blossom island, beyond which stretched the seemingly limitless ice-fields of the Malaspina glacier. All about us the white slope reflected the sunlight with painful brilliancy, while the black moraines and forests below and the mists over the distant ocean, made it seem as if one was looking down into a lower and darker world.

As we advanced toward the head of the glacier we found, as on several subsequent occasions, that the nearer we approached the sources of an ice-stream the easier our progress became. Following up the center of the glacier, we learned that it curved toward the east; and after an hour or two of weary tramping we reached the great amphitheatre in which it has its source. All about us were rugged mountain slopes, heavily loaded with snow, and forming clear white cliffs from which avalanches had descended. To the westward the wall of the amphitheatre was broken, and it was apparent that we could cross its rim in that direction. Pressing onward up the gently ascending slope, we came at length to a gap in the mountains bordered on the north by a towering cliff fully a thousand feet high, and were rejoiced to find that the snow surface on the opposite side of the divide inclined westward with a grade as gentle as the one we had ascended. Looking far down the western snow-slope, we could see where it joined a large glacier flowing southward past the end of the great cliffs which extended westward from the divide. The glacier we saw in the valley below is designated on our map as the *Seward glacier*, in honor of William H. Seward, the former Secretary of State, who negotiated the purchase of Alaska for the United States.

(129)

The pass we named *Pinnacle pass*, on account of the many towering pinnacles overshadowing it. Its elevation is about four thousand feet, and at the summit it has a breadth of only two or three hundred feet. The snow on the divide is greatly crevassed, but a convenient snow-bridge enabled us to cross without difficulty. The crevasses increased in breadth with the advance of the season, and on returning from our mountain trip in September we had to climb up on the bordering cliff in order to pass the main crevasse at the summit. Some idea of the crevasses of this region may be obtained from the following figure, drawn from a photograph taken on the western side of Pinnacle pass, not far from the summit.

FIGURE 5—*Crevasses on Pinnacle Pass; from a Photograph.*

The cliff on the north of Pinnacle pass is really a huge fault-scarp of recent date, intersecting stratified shale, limestone, and conglomerate, with a few thin coal-seams. The strata dip toward the north at a high angle, and present their broken edges in the great cliff rising above the pass. The cliffs extend westward from the pass, and retain a nearly horizontal crest line, but increase in height and grandeur, owing to the downward grade of the glacier along their base. A mile to the westward their elevation is fully two thousand feet. The cliffs throughout are almost everywhere bare of snow and too steep and rugged to be scaled. They form a strongly drawn boundary line in the geology of the region, and furnish the key to the structure and geological character of an extended area. All the rocks to the southward are sandstone and shale belonging to a well-defined series, and differ materially from the rocks in the fault-scarp. I have called the rocks toward the south, the *Yakutat system*, and those exposed in the faces of the fault-scarp the *Pinnacle system*. Directly north of Pinnacle pass, and at the base of Mount Owen, the rocks of the Yakutat system are exposed, and from their position and association it is evident that they are younger than the Pinnacle system and belong above it. If these conclusions are sustained by future investigation, they will carry with them certain deductions which are among the most remarkable in geological history. On the crest of the Pinnacle pass cliffs I afterwards found strata containing fossil shells and leaves belonging to species still living. These records of animal and plant life show that not only were the rocks of the Pinnacle system deposited since living species of mollusks and plants came into existence, but that the Yakutat system is still more recent. More than this, the upheaval of the mountains, the formation of numerous fault-scarps, and the origin of the glaciers, have all occurred since Pliocene times.

The discovery of Pinnacle pass left no question as to the route to be traversed in order to reach the mountains to the westward. We returned to Camp 12, and the following day, with Crumback and Lindsley to assist us, advanced our camp across Pinnacle pass and far down the western snow-slope.

The day we crossed the pass was bright and clear in the morning, but clouds gathered around all the higher peaks about midday, vanishing again at nightfall. As it was desirable to occupy, for topographic and other purposes, a station on the top of the cliffs overlooking Pinnacle pass, we made an effort to reach the crest of the ridge by climbing up the steep scarp just at the divide, where the cliffs are lowest. While Crumback returned to Camp 12 for an additional load and Lindsley went ahead to discover a new camping place, Kerr and myself, taking the necessary instruments, began the ascent; but we found it exceedingly difficult. The outcrops of shale in the lower portion of the cliff furnished but poor foothold, and crumbled and broke away at every step. Once my companion, losing his support, slid slowly down the slope in spite of vigorous efforts to hold on, and a rapid descent in the yawning chasm below seemed inevitable, when, coming to a slightly rougher surface, he was able to control his movements and to regain what had been lost. Climbing on, we came to the base of a vertical wall of shale several hundred feet high, and made a detour to the left where a cascade plunged down a narrow channel. We ascended the bed of the stream, which was sometimes so steep that the spray dashed over us, and reached the base of an overhanging cliff of conglomerate composed of well-worn pebbles. Above this rose a cliff of snow fifty feet or more in height, which threatened to crash down in avalanches at any moment. One small avalanche did occur during the ascent, and scattered its spray in our faces. Had a heavy avalanche formed, our position would have been exceedingly dangerous; but by taking advantage of every overhanging ledge, and watching for the least sign of movement in the snow above, we reached without accident a sheltered perch underneath an overhanging cliff near the base of the snow. We then discovered that clouds were forming on all the high mountains, and shreds of vapor blown over the crest of the cliff above told us that further efforts would be useless. Seeking a perch protected from avalanches by an overhanging cliff, we had a splendid view far out over the sloping snow-plain toward the west and of the mountains bordering Pinnacle pass on the south. My notes written in this commanding station read as follows:

" Looking down from my perch I can plainly distinguish the undulations and crevasses in the broad snow-fields stretching westward from Pinnacle pass. Each inequality in the rock beneath the glacier is reproduced in flowing and subdued outlines in the white surface above. The positions of bosses and cliffs in the rock beneath are indicated by rounded domes and steep descents in the snow surface. About the lower sides of these inequalities there are in some cases concentric blue lines and in others radiating fissures, marking where the snow has broken in making the descent. The side light shining from the eastward down the long westerly slope reveals by its delicate shading the presence of broad, terrace-like, transverse steps into which the stream is divided. Were the snow removed and the rock beneath exposed, we should find broad terraces separated by scarps sweeping across the bed of the glacier from side to side. Similar terraces occur in glaciated cañons in the Rocky Mountains and the Sierra Nevada, but their origin has never been explained. The glacier is here at work sculpturing similar forms; but still it is impossible to understand how the process is initiated.

"Right in front of us, and only a mile or two away, rise the cliffs, spires, and pinnacles of the Hitchcock range. Every ravine and amphitheatre in the great mountain mass is deeply filled with snow, and the sharp angular crests look as if they had been thrust up through the general covering of white. The northern end of the range is clearly defined by the east-and-west fault to which Pinnacle pass owes its origin. The trend of the mighty cliffs on the southern face, on which we have found a perch, is at right angles to the longer axis of the Hitchcock range, and marks its northern terminus both topographically and geologically.

"There is not even a suggestion of vegetation in sight. The eye fails to detect a single dash of green or the glow of a single Alpine flower anywhere on the rugged slopes. A small avalanche from the snow-cliffs above, cascading over the cliff which shelters me and only a few yards away, tells why the precipices are so bare and desolate: they have been swept clean by avalanches.

"Far down the western snow-slope I can distinguish crevasses and dirt bands in the Seward glacier, which flows southward past the range on which we sit. The marginal crevasses along the border of the glacier can clearly be distinguished. As usual, they trend up-stream and, meeting medial crevasses, break the surface of the glacier into thousands of pinnacles and tables. Along the center of the stream there are V-shaped dirt bands, separated by crevasses, which point down-stream and give the appearance of a rapid flow to the central portion of the glacier. From this distance its center has the appearance of 'watered' ribbon.

"A little toward the south of where the medial crevasses are most numerous, and at a locality where two opposite mountain spurs force the ice-stream through the comparatively narrow gorge, there is evidently an ice-fall, as the whole glacier from side to side disappears from view. The appearance of Niagara when seen from the banks of the river above the Horseshoe falls is suggested. Beyond this silent cataract, the eye ranges far out over the broad, level surface of the Malaspina glacier, and traces the dark morainal ribbons streaming away for miles from the mountain spurs among which they originate. From the extreme southern cape of the Samovar hills there is a highly compound moraine-belt stretching away toward the south, and then dividing and curving both east and west. The central band of débris must be a mile broad. Along its eastern margin I can count five lesser bands separated by narrow intervals of ice, and on the farther side similar secondary bands are suggested, but the height of the central range almost completely conceals them from view. In the distant tattered ends, however, their various divisions can be clearly traced. Great swirls in the ice are there indicated by concentric curves of débris on its surface.

"Still farther westward there are hills rising to the height of impressive mountains, in which northward dipping rocks, apparently of sandstone and shale, similar to those forming the Hitchcock range, are plainly distinguishable. All the northern slopes of these hills are deeply buried beneath a universal covering of snow evidently hundreds of feet thick, which is molded upon them so as to reveal every swelling dome and ravine in their rugged sides. Farther westward still, beyond a dark headland apparently washed by the sea, there are other broad ice-fields of the same general character as the Malaspina glacier, which stretch away for miles and miles and blend in the dim distance with the haze of the horizon.

"Just west of the Seward glacier, and in part forming its western shore, there are dark, rocky crests projecting through the universal ice mantle, suggesting the lost mountains of Utah and Nevada which have become deeply buried by the dusts of the desert. The character of the sharp crests beyond the Seward glacier indicate that they are the upturned edges of fault-blocks similar to the one on which we are seated. Interesting geological records are there waiting an interpreter. The vastness of the mountains and the snow-fields to be seen at a single glance from this point of view can scarcely be realized. There are no familiar objects in sight with which to make eye-measurements; the picture is on so grand a scale that it defies imagination's grasp."

Searching the snow-sheet below with a field-glass, I discover a minute spot on the white surface. Its movement, slow but unmistakable, assures me that it is Lindsley returning from the site chosen for our camp to-night. Although apparently near at hand, he forms but an inconspicuous speck on the vast snow-field.

Having learned all that I could of the geology of the cliff, and the gathering clouds rendering it unnecessary to climb the summits above, we descended with even more difficulty than we had encountered on our way up, and met Lindsley as he reached the pass. Resuming our packs, we started on, knowing that Crumback would follow our trail; and after two hours' hard tramping over a snow surface rendered somewhat soft by the heat of the day, but fortunately little crevassed, we reached the place chosen for our camp. Crumback soon joined us, and we pitched our tent for the night. The place chosen was on a little island of débris, the farthest out we could discover from the base of the great cliff on the north. We judged that we should there be safe from avalanches, although the screech and hiss of stones falling from the cliff were heard many times during the night.

Lindsley and Crumback, on revisiting the site of our camp two days later, found that a tremendous avalanche of snow and rocks had in the mean time fallen from the cliffs and ploughed its way out upon the glacier to within fifteen or twenty feet of where we had passed the night. They remarked that if the avalanche had occurred while we were in camp, our tent would not have been reached, but that we should probably have been scared to death by the roar.

First full View of St. Elias.

Leaving Crumback and Lindsley to make our camp as comfortable as possible, Kerr and I pressed on with the object of seeing all we could of the country ahead before the afternoon sunlight faded into twilight. Mount St. Elias had been shut out from view, either by clouds or by intervening mountains, for several days; but it was evident that on approaching the end of the Pinnacle pass fault-scarp we should behold it again, and comparatively near at hand.

Continuing down the even snow-slope, in which there were but few crevasses, the view became broader and broader as we advanced, and at length the great pyramid forming the culminating summit of all the region burst into full view. What a glorious sight! The great mountain seemed higher and grander and more regularly proportioned than any peak I had ever beheld before. The white plain formed by the Seward glacier gave an even foreground, broken by crevasses which, lessening in perspective, gave distance to the foot-hills forming the western margin of the glacier. Far above the angular crest of the Samovar hills in the middle distance towered St. Elias, sharp and clear against the evening sky. Midway up the final slope a thin, horizontal bar of gray clouds was delicately penciled. Through the meshes of the fairy scarf shone the yellow sunset sky. The strong outlines of the rugged mountain, which had withstood centuries of storms and earthquakes, were softened and glorified by the breath of the summer winds, chilled as they kissed its crystal slopes.

Could I give to the reader a tithe of the impressions that such a view suggests, they would declare that painters had never shown them mountains, but only hills. So majestic was St. Elias, with the halo of the sunset about his brow, that other magnificent peaks now seen for the first time or more fully revealed than ever before, although worthy the respect and homage of the most experienced mountain-climber, scarcely received a second glance.

Returning to camp, we passed the night, and the following day, August 6, advanced our camp to the eastern border of the Seward glacier at the extreme western end of the upturned crest forming the northern wall of Pinnacle pass.

The western end of the Pinnacle pass cliff is turned abruptly northward, and the rocks dip eastward at a high angle, showing, together with other conditions, that the end of the ridge is determined by a cross-fault running northeast and southwest. West of the Seward glacier there is a continuation of the Pinnacle-pass cliff, but it is greatly out of line. The position of the Seward glacier, in this portion of its course, was determined by the fault which broke the alignment of the main displacement.

Many facts of similar nature show that the glaciers of the St. Elias region have had their courses determined, to a large extent, by the faults which have given the region its characteristic structure; the ice drainage is consequent to the structure of the underlying rocks; the glaciers not only did not originate the channels in which they flow, but have failed to greatly modify them.

Camp 14 was on a sharp crest of limestone, conglomerate, and shale belonging to the Pinnacle system, which was not over ten feet broad where our tent was pitched. East of our tent there was a broad, upward sloping snow-plain banked against the precipitous base of a hill about a thousand feet high. At the edge of the snow, within three feet of our tent, there was a pond of clear water, seemingly placed there for our special use. The western edge of our tent was at the margin of a cliff about a hundred feet high, overlooking the Seward glacier. We held this camp for several days and reoccupied it on our return from St. Elias.

SUMMIT OF PINNACLE PASS CLIFFS.

From Camp 14 Crumback returned to Blossom island, and Stamy took his place. Word from Christie assured me that supplies would be advanced to Blossom island, and that our cache on the Marvine glacier would be renewed. Stamy's arrival was especially welcome for the reason that he brought letters from dear ones far away, which had been forwarded from Sitka by a trading schooner that chanced to visit Yakutat bay.

While the camp hands were busy in bringing up fresh supplies, Kerr and I occupied two stations on the summit of the Pinnacle pass cliffs. One of these was on a butte at the western end of the ridge and just above our camp; the other was on the crest of the main line of cliffs almost directly above Pinnacle pass, at an elevation of 5,000 feet. Each of the stations embraced magnificent views, extending from the outer margin of the Malaspina glacier to the crest of the St. Elias range. The station on the butte near camp was occupied several times, and proved to be a most convenient and commanding point for study of the geography, geology, and distribution of glacier over a wide area. On account of the splendid view obtained from the top we named it *Point Glorious.* Its elevation is 3,500 feet.

One of the days on which we occupied Point Glorious was especially remarkable on account of the clearness and freshness of the air and the sharpness with which each peak and snow-crest stood out against the deep-blue heavens. We left our camp early in the morning, and spent several hours on the summit. On our way up we found several large patches of Alpine flowers and, under a tussock of moss, a soft, warm nest just abandoned by a mother ptarmigan with her brood of little ones. One hundred feet higher we came to the borders of the snow-field which covered all of the upper slopes except a narrow crest of sandstone at the top.

The Seward glacier, sweeping down from the northeast, curves about the base of Point Glorious and flows on southward. Its surface has the appearance of a wide frozen river. Toward the east of our station there was a broad, level-floored amphitheatre, bounded on the south by the cliffs of Pinnacle pass and on the east by long snow-slopes which stretch up the gorges in the side of Mount Cook. The amphitheatre opens toward the northwest, and discharges its accumulated snows into the Seward glacier. Beyond this, on the north, stood the great curtain-wall named the Corwin cliffs, west of which rose Mount Eaton, Mount Augusta, Mount Malaspina, and other giant summits of the main St. Elias range. Toward the west the view culminated in St. Elias itself, ruggedly outlined against the sky. As the reader will become more and more familiar with the magnificent scenery of the St. Elias region as we advance, it need not be described in detail at this time.

All day the skies were clear and bright, giving abundant opportunity for making a detailed survey of the principal features in view, and for reading the history written in cliffs and glaciers. When the long summer day drew to a close, we returned to our tent and watched the great peaks become dim and generalized in outline as the twilight deepened. The fading light caused the mountains to recede farther and farther, until at last they seemed ghostly giants, too far away to be definitely recognized. With the twilight came soft, gray, uncertain clouds drawn slowly and silently about the rugged precipices by the summer winds from the sea. St. Elias became enveloped in luminous clouds, with the exception of a few hundred feet of the shining summit ; and a glory in the sky, to the left of the veiled Saint, marked the place where the sun went down. The shadows crept across the snow-fields and changed them from dazzling white to a soft gray-blue. Night came on silently, and with but little change. There was no folding of wings ; no twittering of birds in leafy branches ; no sighing of winds among rustling leaves. All was stern and wild and still ; there was not a touch of life to relieve the desolation. A midwinter night in inhabited lands was never more solemn. Man had never rested there before.

The air grew chill when the shadows crossed our tent, and delicate ice crystals began to shoot on the still surface of our little pond. We bade good night to the stern peaks, about which there were signs of a coming storm, and sought the shelter of our tent. Small and comfortless as was that shelter, it shut out the wintry scene and afforded a welcome retreat. Sound, refreshing sleep, with dreams of loved ones far away, renewed our strength for another advance.

The next day, August 8, a topographic station was occupied on the summit of the Pinnacle pass cliffs. We were astir before sunrise, and had breakfast over before four o'clock. The morning was cold, and a cutting wind swept down the Seward glacier from the northeast. All of the mountains were lost to view in dense clouds. A few rays of sunshine breaking through the vapor banks above Point Glorious gave promise of better weather during the day. Lindsley and Stamy had not yet returned from the lower camp, where they were to obtain additional rations; and Kerr and I concluded to try to reach the crest of the Pinnacle pass cliffs and take the chances of the weather being favorable for our work.

Leaving camp in the early morning light, we chose to climb over the summit of Point Glorious rather than thread the crevasses at its northern base. Reaching the top of the point, we were still beneath the low canopy of clouds, and could see far up the great amphitheatre to the base of *Mount Owen*.[*] Descending the eastern slope, we soon reached the floor of the amphitheatre, and found the snow smooth and hard and not greatly crevassed. Cheered by faint promise of blue skies, we pressed on rapidly, the snow creaking beneath our tread as on a winter morning. Two or three hours of rapid walking brought us to the southern wall of the amphitheatre, nearly beneath the point we wished to occupy. As we ascended the slope the way became more difficult, owing not only to its steepness but also to the fact that the snow was softening, and also because great crevasses crossed our path. Looking back over the snow we had crossed, two well-characterized features on its surface could be distinguished: these were large areas with a gray tint, caused by a covering of dust. This dust comes from the southern faces of the Pinnacle pass cliffs, and is blown over the crest of the ridge and scattered far and wide over the snow-fields toward the north. Should the dust-covered areas become buried beneath fresh snow, it is evident that the strata of snow would be separated by thin layers of darker color. This is what has happened many times, as we could see by looking down into the crevasses. In one deep gulf I counted five distinct strata of clear white snow, separated by narrow dust-bands. In other instances there are twenty or more such strata visible. Each layer is evidently the record of a snow-storm, while the dust-bands indicate intervals of fine weather.

[*] Named for David Dale Owen, United States geologist.

The strata of snow exposed to view in the crevasses, after being greatly compressed, are usually from ten to fifteen feet thick, but in one instance exceeded fifty feet. If we assume that each layer represents a winter's snow, and that compression has reduced each stratum to a third of its original thickness (and probably the compression has been greater than this), it is evident that the fresh snows must sometimes reach the depth of from 50 to 150 feet.

Toiling on up the snow-slope, we had to wind in and out among deep crevasses, sometimes crossing them by narrow snow-bridges, and again jumping them and plunging our alpenstocks deep in the snow when we reached the farther side. After many windings we reached the summit of the Pinnacle-pass cliffs. The crest-line is formed of an outcrop of conglomerate composed of sand and pebbles, in one layer of which I found large quantities of mussel shells standing in the position in which the creatures lived. The present elevation of this ancient sea-bottom is 5,000 feet. The strata incline northward at angles of 30° to 40°. All of the northern slope of the ridge is deeply covered with snow, and the rock only appears along the immediate crest. There are, in fact, two crests, as is common with many mountain ridges in this rigion, one of rock and the second of snow; the snow crest, which is usually the higher, is parallel to the rock crest and a few rods north of it. In the valley between the two ridges we found secure footing, and ascended with ease to the highest point on the cliffs. Looking over the southern or rocky crest, we found a sheer descent of about 1,500 feet to the snow-fields below.

The clouds diminished in density and gradually broke away, so that the entire extent of the St. Elias range was in view, with the exception of the crowning peak of all, which was still veiled from base to summit. A spur of St. Elias, extending southward from the main peak, and named *The Chariot*, gleamed brightly in the sunlight. It was the first point on which we made observations. Stretching eastward from St. Elias is the sharp crest of the main range, on which stand Mounts Newton, Jeannette, Malaspina, Augusta, Logan, and several other splendid peaks not yet named. Just to the right of Mount Augusta, on the immediate border of the Seward glacier, rise the Corwin cliffs, marking an immense fault-scarp of the same general character as the one on which we stood.

Mr. Kerr endeavored at first to occupy a station on the crest of the rocky ridge, but as the steepness of the slope and the shattered condition of the rock rendered the station hazardous, the snow-ridge, which was covered with dust and sand and nearly as firm as rock, was occupied instead. The clouds parting toward the northeast revealed several giant peaks not before seen, some of which seem to rival in height St. Elias itself. One stranger, rising in three white domes far above the clouds, was especially magnificent. As this was probably the first time its summit was ever seen, we took the liberty of giving it a name. It will appear on our maps as *Mount Logan*, in honor of Sir William E. Logan, founder and long director of the Geological Survey of Canada.

The clouds grew denser in the east, and shut off all hope of extending the map-work in that direction. While Kerr was making topographic sketches I tried to decipher some of the geological history of the region around me and make myself more familiar with its glaciers and snow-fields.

Even more remarkable than the mighty peaks toward the north, beheld that day for the first time, was the vast plateau of ice stretching seaward from the foot of the mountains. From my station what seemed to be the ocean's shore near Icy bay could just be distinguished. Beyond the bay there is a group of hills which come boldly down to the sea, and apparently form a sea-cliff at the water's edge. Beyond this headland there is another vast glacier extending westward to the limits of vision. The view from this point is essentially the same as that obtained from the cliffs at Pinnacle pass a few days earlier, except that it is far more extended. It need not be described in detail.

The clouds becoming thicker and settling in dark masses about the mountains, we gave up all hope of further work and started for our camp. On the way down the ridge between the crest of snow and the crest of rock we found a stratum of sandstone filled with fossil leaves, and near at hand another layer charged with very recent sea-shells. Collecting all of these that we could carry, we trudged on, finding the snow soft and some of the bridges which we had easily crossed in the morning now weak, trembling, and insecure. We crossed them safely, however, and, reaching the level floor of the amphitheatre, marched wearily on toward Point Glorious. This time we passed along the northern base of the butte at an elevation of two or three hundred feet above the glacier, and, taking a convenient slide down the snow-slope, reached our tent.

Soon a delicious cup of coffee was prepared, bacon was fried, and these were put in a warm place while some griddle cakes were being baked. A warm supper, followed by a restful pipe, ended the day. Kerr and I were our own cooks and our own housekeepers during much of the time we lived above the snow-line. We cleared away the remains of the supper, and prepared our blankets for the night. One of the huge ice pinnacles on the glacier fell with a great crash just as we were turning in. Rain began to fall, and the night was cold and disagreeable; how it passed I do not know, as I slept soundly. Scarcely anything less serious than the blowing away of our tent could have awakened me.

Across Seward Glacier to Dome Pass.

Stormy weather and the necessity of bringing additional supplies from Blossom island detained us at Camp 14 until August 13. We rose at three o'clock on the morning of that day, and, after a hasty breakfast, prepared to cross the Seward glacier. The morning was cold but clear, and the air was bracing. Each peak and mountain crest in the rugged landscape stood out boldly in the early light, although the sun had not risen. Soon the summit of St. Elias became tipped with gold, and then peak after peak, in order of their rank, caught the radiance, and in a short time the vast snow-fields were of dazzling splendor.

The frost of the night before had hardened the snow, which made walking a pleasure. We crossed a rocky spur projecting northward from Point Glorious into the Seward glacier, and had to lower our packs down the side of the precipice with the aid of ropes. Our course led at first up the border of the great glacier to a point above the head of the rapids already referred to, then curved to the westward, and for a mile or two coincided with the general trend of the crevasses. We made good progress, but at length we came to where the Augusta glacier pours its flood of ice into the main stream and, owing to its high grade, is greatly broken. Skirting this difficult area, we passed a number of small blue lakelets and reached the western border of the Seward glacier. We found a gently rising snow-slope leading westward through a gap that could be seen in hills a few miles in advance. But little difficulty was now experienced, except that the snow had become soft under the summer's sun, and walking over it with heavy loads was wearisome in the extreme. We could see, however, that the way ahead was clear, and that encouraged us to push on. Toward night we found a camping place on a steep ridge of shale and sandstone projecting eastward from a spur of Mount Malaspina. This ridge rises about five hundred feet above the surrounding glacier, and has steep roof-like slopes. The summer sun had melted nearly all the snow from its southern face, but the northern slope was still heavily loaded. The snow on the northern side stood some thirty or forty feet higher than the rocky crest of the ridge itself, and between the rock crest and the snow crest there was a little valley which afforded ample shelter for our tent and was quite safe from avalanches. The melting of the snow-bank during the warm days supplied us with water.

The formation of crests of snow standing high above the rocky ridges on which they rest is a peculiar and interesting feature of the mountains of the St. Elias region. A north-and-south section through the ridge on which Camp 15 was situated, exhibiting the double crests, one of rock and the other of snow, is shown at *a* in figure 6. *b* is a section through a similar ridge with a still

Figure 6—*Snow Crests on Ridges and Peaks; from Field Sketches.*

higher snow crest. The remaining figures in the illustration are sketches of mountain peaks, as seen from the south, which have been increased in height by a heavy accumulation of snow on their northern slopes. These sketches are of peaks among the foothills of Mount Malaspina, and show snow pinnacles from fifty to more than a hundred feet high. In some instances, domes and crests of snow were seen along the western sides of the ridges and peaks, but as a rule these snow-tips on the mountains are confined to their northern slopes. The edges and summits of the snow-ridges are sharply defined and clearly cut. The southern slope exposed above the crest of rock is often concave, while the northern slopes are usually convex.

In climbing steep ridges the double crests are frequently of great assistance. Safe footing may frequently be found in the channels between the crests of rock and snow, by the aid of which very precipitous peaks may be climbed with ease. In case the ascent between the two crests is not practicable, the even snow-slope itself affords a sure footing for one used to mountain climbing.

After establishing Camp 15, Lindsley and Stamy returned to one of the lower camps for additional supplies, while Kerr and I explored a way for farther advance.

Our camp occupied a commanding situation. From the end of the ridge on which it was located there was a splendid view of glaciers and mountains to the eastward. The illustration forming plate 18 is from a photograph taken from that station. Toward the north, and only a few miles away, rose the bare, rugged slope of Mount Malaspina. In a wild, high-grade gorge on its western side, a glacier, all pinnacles and crevasses, tumbles down into the broad white plain below. On account of its splendid ice-fall this was named the *Cascade glacier*. Beyond the white plain, stretching eastward for fifteen or twenty miles, there rise the foothills of Mount Cook. Farther south, the rugged, angular summits of the Hitchcock range are in full view, and toward the north stands *Mount Irving*,* which rivals even Mount Cook in the symmetrical proportions of its snow-covered slopes.

The surface of the vast snow-plain near at hand is gashed by many gaping fissures, but the distance is so great that these minor details disappear in a general view. Looking down over the snow, one may see the crevasses as in a diagram. They look as if the white surface had been gashed with a sharp knife, and then stretched in such a way as to open the cuts. That the snow of the névés may be stretched, at least to a limited extent, is shown by the character of these fissures. The crevasses are widest in the center and come to a point at their curving extremities. Two crevasses frequently overlap at their ends and leave a sliver of ice stretching across diagonally between them. It is by means of these diagonal bridges that one is enabled to thread his way through the crevasses.

On returning to camp in the evening, weary with a hard day's climb, a never-failing source of delight was found in the matchless winter landscape to the eastward. The evenings following days of uninterrupted sunshine were especially delightful. The blue shadows of the western peaks creeping across the shining surface were nearly as sharp in outline as the peaks that cast

---

* Named in honor of Professor Roland Duer Irving, U. S. geologist.

them. When the chill of evening made itself felt, and the dropping water and the indefinite murmurs from the glacier below were stilled, the silence became oppressive. The stillness was so profound that it seemed as though the footsteps of the advancing shadows should be audible.

On warm sunny days, however, there are noises enough amid the mountains. The snow, partially melted and softened by the heat, falls from the cliffs in avalanches that make the mountains tremble and, with a roar like thunder, awaken the echoes far and near. During our stay at Camp 15 the avalanches were sometimes so frequent on the steep mountain faces toward the north that the roar of one falling mass of snow and rocks was scarcely hushed before it was succeeded by another.

On the southward-facing cliffs of Mount Augusta, composed of schist which disintegrates rapidly, there are frequent rock avalanches. A rock or a mass of comminuted schist sometimes breaks away even in midday, although these avalanches occur most frequently when the moisture in the rocks freezes. The midday avalanches, I fancy, may be started by the expansion of the rocks owing to the sun's heat. A few stones dislodged high up on the cliffs fall, and, loosening others in their descent, soon set in motion a train of dirt and stones, which flows down the steep ravines with a long rumbling roar, at the same time sending clouds of dust into the air. If the wind is blowing up the cliffs, as frequently happens on warm days, the dust is carried far above the mountains, and hangs in the air like clouds of smoke.

It has been frequently stated that St. Elias is a volcano, and sea captains sailing on the Pacific have seen what they supposed to be smoke issuing from its summit. As its southern face is composed of the same kind of rocks and is of the same precipitous nature as the southern slope of Mount Augusta, it appears probable that what was supposed to be volcanic smoke was in reality avalanche dust blown upward by ascending air currents.

The disintegration of the mountain summits all through the St. Elias region is so great that one constantly wonders that anything is left; yet, except late in the fall, the snow surfaces at the bases of even the steepest cliffs are mostly bare of débris. The absence of earth and stones on the surfaces of the névé fields is mainly due, of course, to the fact that these are regions of accumulation where the winter's snow exceeds the summer's melting.

Thus each year the surface is renewed and made fresh and clean, and any débris that may have previously accumulated is concealed.

There is another reason, however, why but little débris is found at the bases of the steep precipices. The snows of winter are banked high against these walls, but when the rocks are warmed by the return of the summer's sun the snow near their dark surfaces is melted, and leaves a deep gulf between the upward-sloping banks of snow and the sides of the cliffs. These black chasms are frequently 150 or 200 feet deep, and receive all the débris that falls from above. In this way very large quantities of earth and stones are injected, as it were, into the glacier, and only come to light again far down toward the ends of the ice-streams, where the summer's melting exceeds the winter's supply.

On August 14, Kerr and I made an excursion ahead to the border of the Agassiz glacier. The snow-slope south of our camp led westward up a gentle grade to a gap in the hills between two bold, snow-covered domes. The gap through which the snow extended, uniting with a broad snow-field sloping westward, was only a few hundred feet wide, and formed a typical mountain pass, designated on our map as *Dome pass.* Its elevation is 4,300 feet. When near the summit of the pass a few steps carried us past the divide of snow, and revealed to our eager eyes the wonderland beyond. St. Elias rose majestically before us, unobstructed by intervening hills, and bare of clouds from base to summit. We were greatly encouraged by the prospect ahead, as there were evidently no obstacles between us and the actual base of the mountain. A photograph of the magnificent peak was taken, from which the illustration forming plate 19 has been drawn. To the right of the main mountain mass, as shown in the illustration, rises *Mount Newton,*[*] one of the many separate mountain peaks crowning the crest of the St. Elias range. Our way led down the snow-slope in the foreground to the border of the Agassiz glacier, which comes in view between the foot-hills in the middle distance and the sculptured base on which the crowning pyramid of St. Elias stands. After reaching the Agassiz glacier we turned to the right, and made our way to the amphi-

---

[*] Named for Henry Newton, formerly of the School of Mines of Columbia college and author of a report on the geology of the Black hills of Dakota.

MT. ST. ELIAS, FROM DOME PASS.

theatre lying between Mount St. Elias and Mount Newton. On the day we discovered Dome pass, we pressed on down the western snow-slope and reached the side of the Agassiz glacier, which we found greatly crevassed; selecting a camping place on a rocky spur, we returned to Camp 15, and two days later established camp at the place chosen.

Camp 16 was similar in many ways to Camp 14. It had about the same altitude; it was at the western end of a rugged mountain spur, and on the immediate border of a large southward-flowing glacier. On the lower portions of the cliffs, near at hand, there were velvety patches of brilliant Alpine flowers mingled with thick bunches of wiry grass and clumps of delicate ferns. Most conspicuous of all the showy plants, so bright and lovely in the vast wilderness of snow, were the purple lupines. Already the flowers on the lower portions of their spikes had matured, and pods covered with a thick coating of wooly hairs were beginning to be conspicuous. There are no bees and butterflies in these isolated gardens, but brown flies with long-pointed wings were abundant. A gray bird, a little larger than a sparrow, was seen flitting in and out of crevasses near the border of the ice, apparently in quest of insects. Once, while stretched at full length on the flowery carpet enjoying the warm sunlight, a humming bird flashed past me. Occasionally the hoarse cries of ravens were heard among the cliffs, but they seldom ventured near enough to be seen. These few suggestions were all there was to remind us of the summer fields and shady forests in far-away lands.

Up the Agassiz Glacier.

From Camp 16 Kerr and I made an excursion across the Agassiz glacier, while Stamy and Lindsley returned to a lower camp for additional supplies. We found the glacier greatly crevassed and the way across more difficult than on any of the ice-fields we had previously traversed; but by dint of perseverance, and after many changes in our course, we succeeded at last in reaching the western bank, and saw that by climbing a precipice bordering an ice-cascade we could gain a plateau above which we knew from previous observations to be comparatively little broken. We returned to camp, and on August 18 began the ascent of the glacier in earnest. We were favored in the task by brilliant weather.

After reaching the western bank of the glacier, we made our way to the base of the precipice up which we had previously wished to climb. In order to reach it, however, we had to throw our packs across a crevasse over which there was no bridge, and followed them by jumping. The side of the crevasse from which we sprang was higher than its opposite lip, and left us very uncertain as to how we were to return; but that was a matter for the future; our aim at the time was to ascend the glacier, and the return was of no immediate concern.

Reaching the base of the cliff at the side of the glacier, we ascended it without great difficulty, and came out upon the broad plateau of snow above. Thinking that the way onward would be easier along the steep snow-slope bordering the glacier, we made an effort to ascend in that direction, and spent two or three precious hours in trying to find a practicable route. Although the crevasses were fewer than on the glacier proper, yet they were of larger size and had but few bridges. At last we came to a wide gulf on the opposite side of which there was a perpendicular wall of snow a hundred feet high, and all further advance in that direction was stopped. Although obliged to turn back, our elevated position commanded a good view of the glacier below and enabled us to choose a way through the maze of crevasses crossing it. Descending, we plodded wearily on in an irregular zigzag course; but the crevasses became broader and deeper as we advanced, and at length we found ourselves traversing flat table-like blocks of snow, bounded on all sides by crevasses so deep that their bottoms were lost to view. We made our way from one snow-table to another by jumping the crevasses where they were narrowest, or by frail snow-bridges spanning the profound gulfs. Night came on while we were yet in this wild, broken region, and no choice was left us but to pitch our tent in the snow and wait until morning. The night was clear and cold, and a firm crust formed on the snow before morning. Although the temperature was uncomfortable, we were cheered by the prospects of a firm snow surface on the morrow.

We continued our march at sunrise and found the walking easy; but the sun soon came out with unusual brilliancy and softened the snow so much that even the slowest movements were fatiguing. We endeavored to force our way up the center of the glacier through the crevasses and pinnacles of a second ice-fall; but after several hours of exhausting experience we were obliged to change our plan, and endeavored to reach a mountain spur projecting from the western border of the glacier. The sunlight reflected from the snow was extremely brilliant, and the glare from every surface about us was painful to our eyes, already weakened by many days' travel over the white snow. Each member of the party was provided with colored glasses, but in traversing snow-bridges and jumping crevasses these had to be dispensed with. The result was that all of us were suffering more or less from snow-blindness.

About noon we reached the base of the mountain spur toward which our course was bent. It projects into the western border of Agassiz glacier. It is the extension of this cliff underneath the glacier that caused the ice-fall which blocked our way. To go round the end of the cliff with our packs was impracticable, but there seemed a way up the face of the cliff itself, which one could scale by taking advantage of the joints in the rocks. I ascended the snow-slope to the base of the precipice, but found the way upward more difficult than anticipated; and, as the light was very painful to my eyes when not protected by colored glasses, I decided to postpone making the climb until I was in better condition, and in the meantime to see if some other route could not be found. We decided to camp on a small patch of débris near the base of the cliff, and there left our loads. Kerr and Lindsley, taking a rope and alpenstocks, went around the end of the rocky spur and worked their way upward with great difficulty to the top of the cliff immediately above where I had essayed to climb it. A rope was made fast at the top, and our way onward was secured. This place was afterward called *Rope cliff*. The remainder of the afternoon I rested in the tent, with my eyes bound up with tea-leaves, and when evening came found the pain in my head much relieved.

Our tent that night was so near the brink of a crevasse that in order to stay the tent one end of the ridge-rope was made fast to a large stone, which was lowered into the gulf to serve as a stake. Above us rose a precipice nearly a thousand feet high, from which stones were constantly falling; but a deep black gulf intervened between the position we had chosen and the base of the cliffs, and into this the stones were precipitated. Not one of the falling fragments reached the edge of the snow slope on which we were camped, but many times during the night we heard the whiz and hum of the rocks as they shot down from the cliffs.

The noise made by each fragment in its passage through the air increased rapidly in pitch, thus indicating that they were approaching us; but they always fell short of our camp. The bombardment from above was most active just after the shadows fell on the cliffs, showing that the stones were loosened by the freezing of the water in the interstices of the rock.

The next day, August 20, Stamy and Lindsley went back to Camp 16 for more rations, while Kerr and I remained at Camp 18 nursing our eyes and resting. The day passed without anything worthy of note, except the almost constant thunder of avalanches on the mountains. About sunset a dense fog spread over the wintry landscape and threatened to delay the return of the men. When the sun went down, however, the temperature fell several degrees, the mist vanished, and a few stars came out clear and bright. Just as we were about to despair of seeing the men that night we heard a distant shout announcing their return. We had a cup of hot coffee for them when they reached the tent, which they drank with eagerness; but they were too tired to partake of food. Rolling themselves in their blankets, they were asleep in a few minutes.

CAMP ON THE NEWTON GLACIER.

On August 21 we climbed the cliff above Camp 18 by means of the rope already placed there, and found the snow above greatly crevassed. We traveled upward along the steep slope bordering the glacier, but soon came to a deep crevasse which forbade further progress in that direction. Returning to a lower level, we undertook to smooth off an extremely narrow snowbridge so as to make it wide enough to cross, but found the undertaking so hazardous that we abandoned it. By this time it was midday, and we prepared a cup of hot coffee before renewing our attack on the cliffs. After luncheon and a short rest, feeling very much refreshed, we began to cut a series of steps in a bluff of snow about fifty feet high, and made rapid progress in the undertaking. After an hour's hard work one of us reached the top and, planting an alpenstock deep in the snow, lowered a rope to those below. The packs were drawn up one at a time and we were soon ready to advance again.

We found ourselves in a vast amphitheatre bounded on all sides excepting that from which we had come with rugged, snow-covered precipices. The plain was crossed by huge crevasses, some of which were fully a mile in length; but by traveling around their ends or crossing snow-bridges we slowly worked our way onward toward St. Elias. Threading our way through the labyrinth of yawning gulfs, we at last, after the sun had gone down behind the great pyramid toward the west, found a convenient place on the snow, near a blue pond of water, on which to pass the night. Everything was snow-covered in the vast landscape except the most precipitous cliffs, and these were dangerous to approach, owing to the avalanches that frequently fell from them. The weather continued fine. The night was clear and the stars were unusually brilliant. Everything seemed favorable for pushing on. The way ahead presented such even snow-slopes and seemed so free from crevasses that we decided to leave our tent and blankets in the morning and, taking with us as little as possible of impedimenta, endeavor to reach the summit of St. Elias.

Highest Point reached.

Rising at three o'clock on the morning of August 22, we started for the summit of St. Elias, taking with us only our water-proof coats, some food, and the necessary instruments. The higher mountain summits were no longer clearly defined, but in the early light it was impossible to tell whether or not the day was to be fair. From the highest and sharpest peaks, cloud banners were streaming off towards the southeast, showing that the higher air currents were in rapid movement. Vapor banks in the east were flushed with long streamers of light as the sun rose, but soon faded to a dull ashen gray, while the cloud banners between us and the sun became brilliant like the halo seen around the moon when the sky is covered with fleecy clouds. This was the first time in my experience that I had seen colored banners waving from the mountain tops.

We found the snow-surface hard, and made rapid headway up the glacier. Our only difficulty was the uncertainty of the early light, which rendered it impossible to tell the slope of the uneven snow-surfaces. The light was so evenly diffused that there were no shadows. The rare beauty of that silent, wintry landscape, so delicate in its pearly half tones and so softly lighted, was unreal and fairy-like. The winds were still; but strange forebodings of coming changes filled the air. Long, waving threads of vapor were woven in lace-work across the sky; the white-robed mountains were partially concealed by cloud-masses drifting like spirits along their mighty battlements; and far, far above, from the topmost pinnacles, irised banners were signaling the coming of a storm.

We made rapid progress, but early in the day came to the base of a heavy cloud bank which enshrouded all the upper part of St. Elias. Then snow began to fall, and it was evident that to proceed farther would be rash and without promise of success. After twenty days of fatigue and hardship since leaving Blossom island, with our goal almost reached, we were obliged to turn back. Hoping to be able to renew the attempt after the storm had passed, Mr. Kerr left his instruments on the snow between two huge crevasses and we returned to our tent, where we passed the remainder of the day and the night following. The snow continued to fall throughout the day, and the storm increased in force as night came on. When we awoke in the morning the tempest was still raging. We were in the midst of the storm-cloud; the dense vapor and the fine drifting snow-crystals swept along by the wind obscured everything from view; the white snow surface could not be distinguished from the vapor-filled air; there was no earth and no sky; we seemed to be suspended in a white, translucent medium which surrounded us like a shroud. The snow was already more than three feet deep about our tent, and to remain longer with the short supply of provisions on hand was exceedingly hazardous, as there seemed no limit to the duration of the storm. A can of rations had been left at Rope cliff, and we decided to return to that place if possible. Resuming our packs, we roped ourselves together and began to descend through the blinding mist and snow which rendered the atmosphere so dense that a man could not be distinguished at a distance of a hundred feet. With only an occasional glimpse of the white cliff around to guide us, we worked our way downward over snow-bridges and between the crevasses. Our ascent through this dangerous region had been slow and difficult, but our descent was still more tedious. All day long we continued to creep slowly along through the blinding storm, and as night approached believed ourselves near the steps cut in a snow-cliff during the ascent, but darkness came before we reached them. Shoveling the snow away as best we could with our hands and

basins, we cleared a place down to the old snow large enough
for our tent and went into camp.

In the morning, August 24, the storm had spent its force and
left the mountains with an immaculate covering, but still partially veiled by shreds of storm-clouds. We found ourselves on
one of the many tables of snow, bounded on all sides by crevasses
of great depth, but not far from the snow-cliff where we had cut
steps. The steps were obliterated by the new snow, but by means
of a rope and alpenstocks we made the descent without much
difficulty. The last man to go down, not having the help of
the rope, used two alpenstocks, and descended by first planting
one firmly in the snow and lowering himself as far as he could,
still retaining a firm hold, and then planting the other in the
snow at a lower level and removing the higher one. By slowly
and carefully repeating this operation he descended the cliff safely
and rejoined his companions. Passing on beneath the cliffs,
dangerous on account of avalanches, we reached in safety the
precipice where we had left our rope. A heavy avalanche had
swept down from the heights above during our absence and sent
its spray over the precipice we had to descend. The cliff of
ice towering above the place where our rope was fastened had
become greatly melted and honey-combed, and threatened every
moment to crash down and destroy any one who chanced to be
beneath. To stand above the precipice in the shadow of the
treacherous snow-cliffs while the men were descending the rope
was exceedingly trying to one's nerves; but the avalanches did
not come, and the previous camping place below Rope cliff was
reached with safety.

The following day, August 25, after some consultation, it was
decided to once more attempt to reach the top of Mount St.
Elias. Lindsley and Stamy, who had shared without complaint
our privations in the snow, volunteered to descend to a lower
camp for additional rations, while Kerr and myself returned to
the higher camp in the hope that we might be able to ascend
the peak before the men returned, and, if not, to have sufficient
rations when they did rejoin us to continue the attack. The
men departed on their difficult errand, while Kerr and I, with
blankets, tents, oil-stoves, and what rations remained, once more
scaled the cliff where we had placed a rope, and returned on the
trail made the day previously. About noon we reached the excavation in the snow where we had bivouacked in the storm,

and there prepared a lunch. It was then discovered that we had been mistaken as to the quantity of oil in our cans; we found scarcely enough to cook a single meal. To attempt to remain several days in the snow with this small supply of fuel seemed hazardous, and Mr. Kerr volunteered to descend and overtake the men at the lower camp, procure some oil, and return the following day. We then separated, Mr. Kerr starting down the mountain, leaving me with a double load, weighing between sixty and seventy pounds, to carry through the deep snow to the high camp previously occupied.

Alone in the highest Camp.

Trudging wearily on, I reached the high camp at sunset, and pitched my tent in the excavation previously occupied. An alpenstock was used for one tent-pole, and snow saturated with water, piled up in a column, for the other; the snow froze in a few minutes, and held the tent securely. The ends of the ridge-rope were then stamped into the snow, and water was poured over them; the edges of the tent were treated in a similar manner, and my shelter was ready for occupation. After cooking some supper over the oil-stove, I rolled myself in a blanket and slept the sleep of the weary. I was awakened in the morning by snow drifting into my tent, and on looking out discovered that I was again caught in a blinding storm or mist of snow. The storm raged all day and all night, and continued without interruption until the evening of the second day. The coal oil becoming exhausted, a can was filled with bacon grease, in which a cotton rag was placed for a wick; and over this " witch lamp " I did my cooking during the remainder of my stay. The snow, falling steadily, soon buried my tent, already surrounded on three sides by an icy wall higher than my head, and it was only by almost constant exertion that it was kept from being crushed in. With a pint basin for a shovel I cleared the tent as best I could, and several times during the day re-excavated the hole leading down to the pond, which had long since disappeared beneath the level plain of white. The excavation of a tunnel in the snow was also begun in the expectation that the tent would become uninhabitable. The following night it became impossible to keep the tent clear in spite of energetic efforts, and early in the morning it was crushed in by a great weight of snow, leaving me no alternative but to finish my snow-house and move in. A tunnel some four or five feet in length was excavated in the snow, and a chamber about six feet long by four feet wide and three feet high was made at right angles to the tunnel. In this chamber I placed my blankets and other belongings, and, hanging a rubber coat on an alpenstock at the entrance, found myself well sheltered from the tempest. There I passed the day and the night following. At night the darkness and silence in my narrow tomb-like cell was oppressive; not a sound broke the stillness except the distant, muffled roar of an occasional avalanche. I slept soundly, however, and in the morning was awakened by the croaking of a raven on the snow immediately above my head. The grotto was filled with a soft blue light, but a pink radiance at the entrance told that the day had dawned bright and clear.

What a glorious sight awaited me! The heavens were without a cloud, and the sun shone with dazzling splendor on the white peaks around. The broad unbroken snow-plain seemed to burn with light reflected from millions of shining crystals. The great mountain peaks were draped from base to summit in the purest white, as yet unscarred by avalanches. On the steep cliffs the snow hung in folds like drapery, tier above tier, while the angular peaks above stood out like crystals against the sky. St. Elias was one vast pyramid of alabaster. The winds were still; not a sound broke the solitude; not an object moved. Even the raven had gone, leaving me alone with the mountains.

As the sun rose higher and higher and made its warmth felt, the snow was loosened on the steep slopes and here and there broke away. Gathering force as it fell, it rushed down in avalanches that made the mountains tremble and awakened thunderous echoes. From a small beginning high up on the steep slopes, the new snow would slip downward, silently at first, and cascade over precipices hundreds of feet high, looking like a fall of foaming water; then came the roar, increasing in volume as the flowing snow involved new fields in its path of destruction, until the great mass became irresistible and ploughed its way downward through clouds of snow-spray, which hung in the air long after the snow had ceased to move and the roar of the avalanche had ceased. All day long, until the shadow of evening fell on the steep slopes, this mountain thunder continued. The echoes of one avalanche scarcely died away before they were awakened by another roar. To witness such a scene under the most favorable conditions was worth all the privations and anxiety it cost.

Besides the streams of new snow, there were occasional avalanches of a different character, caused by the breaking away of portions of the cliffs of old snow, accumulated, perhaps, during several winters. These start from the summits of precipices, and are caused by the slow downward creep of the snow-fields above. The snow-cliffs are always crevassed and broken in much the same manner as are the ends of glaciers which enter the sea, and occasionally large masses, containing thousands of cubic yards, break away and are precipitated down the slopes with a suddenness that is always startling. Usually the first announcement of these avalanches is a report like that of a cannon, followed by a rumbling roar as the descending mass ploughs its way along. The avalanches formed by old snow are quite different from those caused by the descent of the new surface snow, but are frequently accompanied by surface streams in case there has been a recent storm. The paths ploughed out by the avalanches are frequently sheathed with glassy ice, formed by the freezing of water produced by the melting of snow on account of the heat produced by the friction of the moving mass. A third variety of avalanches, due to falling stones, has already been noticed.

The floor of my snow-chamber was the surface of the old snow on which we had pitched our tents at the time we first reached that camping place. On this hard surface, and forming the walls of the cell, there were thirty inches of clear white snow, the upper limit of which was marked by a blue layer of ice about a quarter of an inch thick. This indicated the thickness of snow that fell during the first storm. Its surface had been melted and softened during the days of sunshine that followed its fall, and had frozen into clear ice. Above the blue band which encircled the upper portion of my chamber was the soft, pure white snow of the second storm. The stratification of snow which I had seen fall rendered it evident that my interpretation of the stratification observed in the sides of crevasses was correct. The snow when it fell was soft and white, and composed of very fine crystals; but under the influence of the air and sunshine it changed its texture and became icy and granular, and then resembled the névé snow so common in high mountains.

The day following the storm was bright and beautiful; the sunlight was warm and pleasant, but the temperature in the shadows was always below freezing. The surface of the snow did not melt sufficiently during the day to freeze and form a crust during the night. It thus became more and more apparent that the season was too far advanced to allow the snow to harden sufficiently for us to be able to climb the mountain. The snow settled somewhat and changed its character, but even at midday the crystals on the surface glittered as brilliantly in the sunlight as they did in the early morning. Although the snow did not melt, its surface was lowered slightly by evaporation. The tracks of the raven, at first sunken a quarter of an inch in the soft surface, after the first day of sunshine stood slightly in relief, but were still clearly defined.

On the sixth day after separating from my companions, judging that they must have returned at least to the camping place where we had separated, I packed my blankets and what food remained, abandoned the tent and oil-stove, and started to descend the mountain. The snow had settled somewhat, but was still soft and yielding and over six feet deep. Tramping wearily on through the chaff-like substance, I slowly worked my way downward, and again threaded the maze of crevasses, now partially concealed by the layer of new snow, with which we had struggled several times before. Midway to the next camping place I met my companions coming up to search for me. Instead of meeting three men, as I expected, I saw five tramping along in single file through the deep snow. The sight of human beings in that vast solitude was so strange that I watched them for some time before shouting. Glad as I was to meet my companions once more, I could not help noticing their rough and picturesque appearance. Each man wore colored glasses and carried a long alpenstock, and two or three had packs strapped on their backs. Several weeks of hard tramping over moraines and snow-fields had made many rents in their clothes, which had been mended with cloth of any color that chanced to be available. Not a few rags were visible fluttering in the wind. To a stranger they would have appeared like a dangerous band of brigands.

The reason for the presence of five men instead of three was this: Lindsley and Stamy, when they left us at Rope cliff to return for additional rations, were obliged to go back to Camp 12 in order to get a tent and an oil-stove. On reaching that place the temptation to return to Blossom island was so great that Lindsley could not resist it and went back to the base-camp, where he reported that Kerr and I were storm-bound in the mountains and in need of assistance. Three men, Partridge, Doney, and White, started at once, and found Stamy, who had waited for their arrival at Camp 12. A day was thus lost, which increased Mr. Kerr's hardship and might have proved disastrous. The party then returned to Rope cliff and joined Kerr on the evening of August 29. On this occasion, as on several others, I found myself indebted to Stamy for willing assistance when others hesitated.

During my imprisonment at the highest camp, Mr. Kerr was detained under similar circumstances at the camp below Rope cliff. On endeavoring to rejoin me with the supply of coal oil, so very valuable under the circumstances, he was caught in the storm and was unable to reach the rendezvous appointed. He reached Rope cliff late in the afternoon of the first day of the storm, climbed the precipice, and found his way through the gathering darkness, along the nearly obliterated trail beneath the avalanche cliffs, and up the steps cut in the snow-cliff, to the site of our bivouac camp. Finding nothing there, and being unable to proceed farther through the blinding storm, he abandoned the attempt and returned to the camp below Rope cliff. In descending the rope, he found that its lower end had become fast in the snow. The taut line, sheathed with ice, was an uncertain help in the darkness. Midway in the descent his hands slipped and he slid to the bottom; but the cushion of new snow broke the fall and prevented serious injury. Alone, without fire, without blankets, having only a canvas cover and a rubber cloth for shelter, and with but little food, he passed three anxious days and nights before the arrival of the camp hands.

THE RETURN.

Deciding that the ascent of Mount St. Elias could not be accomplished through the new snow, which refused to harden, it was decided to abandon the attempt and return to Blossom island. Our retreat was none too soon. Storm succeeded storm throughout September. Each time the clouds lifted, the mantle of new snow was seen to have descended lower and lower. Our last view showed the wintry covering nearly down to timber-line.

On the night of August 31 we slept at the camp beneath Rope cliff, but had a most uncomfortable night. Six men sleeping in a tent measuring seven by seven feet, with but little protection from the ice beneath, certainly does not seem inviting to one surrounded by the comforts of civilization. A large part of the night was occupied by Doney in preparing breakfast over our oil-stove. An early start was welcome to all; we were disappointed at not being able to reach the top of St. Elias, and were anxious to return to more comfortable quarters. Kerr concluded to return at once to Blossom island to recuperate, while I made an excursion up the Seward glacier, with the hope of gaining the upper ice-fall and seeing the amphitheatre beyond.

We left Rope cliff about six in the morning, and found the snow hard and traveling easy for several hours. After descending the lower ice-fall, however, the snow became soft, and a change in the atmosphere indicated the approach of another storm. Kerr and Doney pressed on and were soon lost to sight, while the rest of the party were delayed, owing to Partridge having become snow-blind and almost helpless. As the crevasses were exceedingly numerous and the snow-bridges soft and uncertain, the task of conducting a blind man to a place of safety was by no means light. Partridge bore up bravely under his affliction, however, and did not hesitate in crawling across the treacherous snow-bridges with a rope fastened about his body and a man before and behind to assist his movements. Late in the day we reached our camping place at the eastern border of the Agassiz glacier, while Kerr and Doney crossed Dome pass and spent the night in a tent that had been left standing at the first camping east of the pass. We pitched a tent on our old camping place at Camp 16, and had the luxury of a rocky bed to sleep on that night. As Partridge's blindness still continued, White was sent ahead to tell Kerr and Doney to wait for us in the morning, so that Partridge could accompany them to Blossom island. Rain continued all that night and all the next day. As Partridge's eyes were still unserviceable in the morning, I concluded to wait a day before allowing him to start for Blossom island.

Toward evening on September 21 we moved our camp across

Dome pass, and pitched our tent on the high ridge beside the one occupied by Kerr and Doney. In the morning, although the storm still continued, our party divided, Kerr, Doney, and Partridge starting early for Blossom island, while Stamy, White, and myself, after following their tracks for a few miles, turned to the left and worked our way northeastward among the crevasses of the Seward glacier. Toward evening we reached the northwestern spur of Mount Owen, but found the cliffs rising abruptly from the glacier and too favorable for avalanches to admit of our camping near them. Again we were forced to go into camp on the open glacier, and were less comfortable than previously on similar occasions, owing to the fact that we had been exposed to the rains for three successive days and our blankets and clothes were wet. Rain continued all night and all the next day, and on the following night changed to snow.

On the morning of September 4 we awoke to find the skies clear, but the mountains all about us were white with snow. Before the sun rose, White and I started for the top of the high ridge above us, determined to have at least a distant view of the amphitheatre which we wished to explore. The snow about our camp was only six or eight inches deep, but as we ascended the mountain it grew more and more troublesome, and at a height of a thousand feet above camp was thirty inches deep. On gaining the summit of the ridge a magnificent view was obtained of the upper portion of the Seward glacier and of Mount Irving and Mount Logan, and many bold, tapering mountains farther northeastward. The whole landscape was snow-covered, and as the sun rose clear in the east became of the most dazzling brilliancy. An icy wind swept down from the northeast and rendered it exceedingly difficult to take photographs or to make measurements. On endeavoring to use my prismatic compass, I found that, having been soaked with moisture during the previous days of storm, it froze solid and refused to move, on being exposed to the air. Making what observations I could, we started back to camp with the intention of abandoning all further attempts to work in the high mountains.

On the steep slope now exposed to the full sunshine several avalanches had gone down, and there was great danger of others. Selecting a point where an avalanche had already swept away the new snow, we worked our way downward in a zigzag course and reached the bottom safely, although an avalanche starting near at hand swept by within a few yards. When nearly at the bottom my attention was attracted by a noise above, and on looking up I saw two rocks bounding down the slope and coming straight for me. To dodge them on the steep slippery slope was difficult and dangerous. Allowing one to pass over my right shoulder, I instantly moved in that direction and allowed the other to pass over my left shoulder. They shot by me like fragments of shells, but did no injury. Reaching camp, we found that Stamy had dried our blankets and clothes.

Resuming our packs, we slowly threaded our way downward to Camp 14, at the western end of the Pinnacle pass cliffs. We there found cans of rations left several days before and, pitching our tent, passed the night. We knew by the signs found there that Kerr and his companions, after taking lunch, had renewed their journey toward Blossom island. Our camp was just at the lower limit of the new snow. To the northward all was of the purest white, but southward, down the glacier, the snow-fields were yellow and much discolored. Many changes had taken place in the Seward glacier since we first saw it; the pinnacles, snow-tables, and crevasses in the rapids were less striking than formerly, and had evidently suffered greatly from the summer's heat. About the bases of the cliffs there were dark, irregular patches of débris, where a month previously all was white. As nearly as could be judged, the surface of the glacier had been lowered by melting and settling during our absence about fifty feet.

The following morning, September 5, we started for Blossom island, the weather still continuing thick and stormy. On crossing Pinnacle pass we found over a foot of new snow which had fallen since our companions passed that way. Toward nightfall the lower limit of snow on the Marvine glacier was reached, and at night we camped on the first moraines which appeared below the névé. The day following, September 6, we reached Blossom island about noon, and found that Kerr and his party had arrived there safely, and that Partridge had recovered from his snow-blindness.

Our stay above the snow-line had lasted thirty-five days, and we were extremely glad to see the light of a camp-fire and have the trees and flowers about us once more. The vegetation indicated that the season was already far advanced. Most of the flowers had faded, and autumn tints gave brilliancy to the lower mountain slopes; salmon berries and huckleberries were in profusion, and furnished an exceedingly agreeable change in our diet. After a bath in one of the small lakelets on the island and a good night's rest on a luxuriant bed of spruce boughs, we felt fully restored and ready for another campaign.

As Kerr was anxious to get back to Port Mulgrave, it was arranged that Lindsley and Partridge should go with him, and that the rest of the men should remain. Kerr took his departure on the morning of September 7, and on the following day Christie, Doney, and myself crossed the Marvine glacier to the southern end of the Hitchcock range, and the following day made an excursion out upon the Malaspina glacier. The day of our excursion was bright and beautiful, and the mountains to the northward revealed their full magnificence. The level plateau of ice formed a horizontal plain, from which the mountain rose precipitously and appeared grander and more majestic than from any other point of view. St. Elias rose clear and sharp, without a cloud to obscure its dizzy height, and appeared to be one sheer precipice. It is doubtful if a more impressive mountain face exists anywhere else in the world. After learning all we could concerning the Malaspina glacier we returned to our camp at the end of the Hitchcock range, and the following day tramped across the extremely rough moraine-covered surface back to Blossom island.

The following morning, September 12, we started on our return trip to Yakutat bay. Two small tents and many articles for which we had no further use were abandoned, so as to make our packs light as possible. We crossed the Hayden glacier, and at night camped at the foot of Floral pass. After making two intermediate camps, traveling each day in the rain, we reached the shore of Yakutat bay on September 15.

Doney and I halted at Dalton's cabin for the purpose of seeing what we could of the openings there made for coal, while the rest of the party pressed on to our old camping place on the shore. There they found Kerr and his party still encamped, but ready to leave for Port Mulgrave early the next morning.

September 18 was occupied by us in catching salmon and trout. We were abundantly successful, as every man returned to camp with all that he could carry. These were spread out on a rack over our camp-fire and smoked for further use, as we did not know how long our stay would be extended. On the next day Stamy and Lindsley returned from Port Mulgrave, where they had left Kerr, quite recovered from his exposure on the mountain. Stormy weather continued, and a gale from the northeast piled the ice high on the beach and threatened to sweep away our tents, as has already been briefly described in earlier pages.

On September 20, our tents having been beaten in by a violent storm and our camping place overflowed by the waters from a lake above us, we removed our goods to a place of safety and went to Dalton's cabin, where we awaited better weather. The morning of September 23 dawned clear and bright, and after drying our clothes around a blazing camp-fire, we started back to our camping place on the shore. Before reaching there, however, we were rejoiced to see the *Corwin* coming up the bay. It took us but a short time to get on board, where Captain C. L. Hooper, her commander, did everything in his power to make us welcome and comfortable. To him we are indebted for a delightful voyage back to civilization.

After steaming up Disenchantment bay nearly to the ice-cliffs of the Hubbard glacier, and obtaining a fine view of the glaciers about Disenchantment bay, the *Corwin* returned to Port Mulgrave and, on September 25, put to sea. After a splendid ocean passage, we arrived at Port Townsend on October 2.

During our stay in Alaska not a man was seriously sick and not an accident happened. The work planned at the start was carried out almost to the letter, with the exception that snow-storms and the lateness of the season did not permit us to reach the summit of Mount St. Elias.

SUGGESTIONS.

Should another attempt be made to climb Mount St. Elias, the shortest and most practicable route from the coast would be to land at Icy bay and ascend the Agassiz glacier. The course taken by us in 1890 could be intersected just north of where the tributary glacier from Dome pass joins the main ice-stream ; and from there the route followed last summer would be the most practicable. A camp should be established on the divide between Mount St. Elias and Mount Newton, from which excursions to either of these peaks could be made in a single day.

In the preceding narrative many details have been omitted. One of these is that tents, together with blankets, rations, etc., were left at two convenient points between Blossom island and the Agassiz glacier, and were used by the men in bringing up supplies. In attempting to ascend Mount St. Elias from Icy bay by the route suggested, at least three such relay stations should be established between the Chaix hills, where wood for camp-fires can be obtained (as is known from the reports of the New York *Times* and Topham expeditions), and the high camp on the divide. The relay camps suggested should be one day's march apart, and would serve not only for stopping places while carrying rations during the advance, but would furnish a line of retreat. A party making this journey should be provided with snow-shoes, which unfortunately we did not take with us.

All rations intended for use above the snow-line should be packed in tin cans, each of sufficient size to hold between fifty and sixty pounds, and each should be securely soldered. All articles packed in this way should be thoroughly dry and should be packed in a dry, warm room. When secured in this manner they are about as easy to carry as if packed in bags, and can be "cached" anywhere out of the reach of floods and avalanches, with the certainty of being serviceable when wanted. The more perishable articles to be used where camp-fires are possible should also be secured in tin cans. Sacks of flour, corn-meal, etc., should be protected by an outer covering of strong canvas. The experience of last summer showed that the cans of rations intended for use above the snow-line should each contain about the following ration, which may be varied to suit individual taste:

Bacon, smoked	10	lbs.
Corned beef, in can	6	"
Flour and corn-meal, with necessary quantity of baking powder	15	"
Coffee	2	"
Rolled oats	5	"
Sugar	5	"
Chocolate, sweet	2	"
Salt	1	"
Extract of beef	1	"
Tobacco	½	"
Condensed milk (small cans)	2	
Matches (wax)	1 box.	

Our experience with oil-stoves showed that they are serviceable. While on the march they can be carried as hand packs in gunny-sacks. Rectangular cans holding about a gallon each, with small screw-tops, were found convenient for carrying coal oil. The experience of Arctic explorers indicates that alcohol would perhaps be better than coal oil to use in snow-camps.

Among the most important articles to be provided are strong shoes or boots; of these each man should have at least two pairs. Strong hip-boots, with lacings over the instep, are exceedingly serviceable. When sleeping on the ice the boot-legs may be spread beneath one's blankets and the feet used as a pillow. The long legs are serviceable alike in the thick brush on the shore and in the deep snow on the high mountains. With their protection, many streams can be waded without getting wet. Leather, waxed ends, awls, etc., for repairing boots, and tallow mixed with bees-wax for greasing them, should be taken and distributed in part through the cans of rations. Heavy woolen socks are indispensable, and an effort should be made to have a dry pair always at hand. This may be arranged, even under the most unfavorable conditions, by drying a pair as thoroughly as is convenient and carrying them in the bosom of one's shirt.

Long alpenstocks are always necessary. My own choice is a stiff one of hickory, about six feet long and an inch and a quarter in diameter, provided with a spike and hook at one end and a chisel about two inches broad at the other. Ice axes are desirable while climbing in the high mountains, but even more serviceable are light axes of the usual pattern, but with handles about fourteen inches long; these supplement the alpenstock, and when not actually in use are carried in the packs.

Each man should be provided with a water-tight match-box, and should have, besides, a bundle of wax matches wrapped in oil-cloth and sewed in the collar of his shirt, to be held as a last reserve. Each man should also have a small water-tight bag in which to carry salt enough to last a week or ten days, in case he has to live by hunting or fishing. A heavy hunting knife is very convenient, and can be used not only in cutting trails through thick brush, but in cases of necessity is serviceable in making steps in ice. Heavy woolen clothing is preferable to furs. Sleeping bags were not used during our expedition, but are highly recommended by others. For protection at night, a thick woolen blanket with a light canvas cover and a sheet of light rubber cloth to protect it are all that is necessary. Our tents were of cotton drilling, seven feet square and about six feet high, and provided with ridge-ropes. Alpenstocks were used for tent poles. "Sou'westers" and strong water-proof coats are indispensable in a climate like that of Alaska, and at night may be used as a sub-stratum on which to sleep. While traveling over the snow-line we used colored glasses to protect the eyes, and also found that a strip of dark mosquito netting tied across the face below the eyes afforded great protection. Some of the party found relief from the glare of the snow by blacking their faces with grease and burnt cork, but one experiment with that method is usually enough. While camping below timber-line during the months of June to September fine mosquito netting is indispensable. In carrying packs, hemp "cod-line" of the largest size was found to answer every requirement, and is preferred by expert packers to pack-straps.

It has been suggested that experienced Swiss guides are neces-sary to ensure success in climbing Mount St. Elias. Having never followed a guide in the mountains, I am not able to judge of their efficiency, but it must be remembered that no one can *guide* in a region that has never been traversed. The "guide" as understood in Europe is unknown in America. In the explora-tion of this country by engineers, geologists, etc., the camp hands have followed their leaders and have not shown them the way. In every frontier town there are hunters, trappers, miners, pros-pectors, cow-boys, voyageurs, etc.—men who have passed their lives on the plains or among "the hills" and are enured to hard-ship and danger. This is the best material in the world from which to recruit an exploring party. A foreigner engaging the services of such men must take into account the independent spirit that animates them and is the secret of their usefulness. They are not servants, but retainers; that too in regions far beyond the reach of civil law. They will follow their leader anywhere, support him in all dangers, and do their work faith-fully so long as their rights as men are respected.

By taking proper precautions while traveling across crevassed snow and ice, and guarding against avalanches and snow-blind-ness, an excursion can be made above the snow-line with as little danger as in better known and more frequented regions.

PART III

SKETCH OF THE GEOLOGY OF THE ST. ELIAS REGION.

GENERAL FEATURES.

In the preceding narrative, many references have been made to the character of the rocks and to the geological structure of the region explored. It was not practicable during the journey to carry on detailed geological studies, but such facts as were noted are of interest, for this reason, if for no other: they relate to a country previously unknown.

My reconnoissance enabled me to determine that there are three well-defined formations in the St. Elias region. These are—

1. The sandstones and shales about Yakutat bay and westward along the foot of the mountain to Icy bay, named the *Yakutat system.*

2. A system of probably later date, composed of shale, conglomerate, limestone, sandstone, etc., best exposed in the cliffs of Pinnacle pass and along the northern and western borders of the Samovar hills, and named the *Pinnacle system.*

3. The metamorphic rocks of the main St. Elias range, called the *St. Elias schist.*

YAKUTAT SYSTEM.

The rocks of this system are of gray and brown sandstones and nearly black shales. They are uniform in lithological character over a large area, and are usually greatly crushed and seamed. So great has been the crushing to which they have been subjected that it is difficult to work out a hand specimen with fresh surfaces. Fragments broken out with a hammer are almost invariably bounded by plains of previous crushing, and are usually somewhat weathered.

These rocks form the bold shores of Yakutat and Disenchantment bays, and were the only rocks seen along our route from Yakutat bay to Pinnacle pass. The whole of the Hitchcock range is composed of rocks of this series, as are also the Chaix

(167)

hills and the hills west of Icy bay and the southern portion of
the Samovar hills. North of Pinnacle pass there are rocks undis-
tinguishable lithogically from those about Yakutat bay. These
are exposed in Mount Owen and on each side of Dome pass:
they also form the bold spurs about the immediate bases of
Mount Augusta, Mount Malaspina, and Mount St. Elias. In the
three instances last named these rocks dip beneath the schist
forming the crest of the St. Elias range, and it is probable that a
great overthrust there took place before the formation of the
faults to which the present relief of the mountains is due.

All the mountain spurs of Mount Cook, so far as is known, are
composed of sandstones and shales of the Yakutat series, with
the exception of the Pinnacle pass cliffs. Nearly all the débris
on the glaciers from Disenchantment bay to the Seward glacier,
and probably beyond, is derived from the rocks of this system.
The distribution of the rocks from which the débris was derived
may be ascertained in a general way by tracing out the sources
of the glaciers. Medial moraines on the Hayden and Marvine
glaciers, however, have their sources on the northern slope of
Mount Cook, and are composed of gabbro and serpentine. These
rocks were not seen in place, and their relation to the Yakutat
series can only be conjectured.

Although the rocks of this system are stratified, it is impossible to determine their thickness, for the reason that they have
been greatly crushed and overthrust. This is well illustrated in
the Hitchcock range, which, as already explained, trends about
northeast and southwest, and is composed of strata of shale and
sandstone, having a nearly east-and-west strike and a uniform
dip toward the northeast. Were the rocks in normal position
their thickness would be incredible. In addition to this negative evidence, there is the crushed condition of the strata to show
that movement has taken place all through their mass; and in
a few instances thrust faults were distinguished, dipping northeastward at about the same angle as the lines of bedding. In
the crushing to which the rocks have been subjected the shales
have suffered more than the sandstones, and have been drawn
out into wedge-shaped masses, the sharp edges of which usually
point toward the northeast, which is presumably the direction
from which the crushing force acted.

The hypothesis that the rocks in the St. Elias region have
been crushed and overthrust explains many otherwise inhar-

monious facts, and accounts for the superposition of the St. Elias schist upon rocks of the Yakutat system.

Coal has been discovered in the rocks of the Yakutat system about two miles west of the southern end of Disenchantment bay, and is reported to be of workable thickness. I saw thin lignite seams at the surface at this locality, but as the shafts were filled with water I was unable to examine the coal in the openings, and cannot vouch for its thickness. Samples obtained from the mine show it to be a black lignite which would apparently be of value for fuel. Fossil leaves are reported to occur in connection with the lignite, but these have never been seen by any one who could identify them.

The rocks of the Yakutat system, wherever seen, dip northeastward, except when greatly disturbed near fault-lines. East of Disenchantment bay the inclination of the beds is from 15° to 20°; farther westward the dip increases gradually all the way to the Hitchcock range, where the prevailing inclination is from 30° to 40°, and frequently still greater. Beneath Mount Malaspina and Mount St. Elias the Yakutat sandstones dip northeastward at an angle of about 15°, and in the hills west of Icy bay the dip is about the same. Exceptions to the prevailing dips occur along the immediate shore of Yakutat bay, northwest of Knight island, and at the southern extremity of each of the mountain spurs between Yakutat bay and Blossom island. At these localities the rocks are frequently vertical or nearly so, owing their high dip to the proximity of lines of displacement. The faults indicated by these unusual dips also mark the boundary between the mountains and the seaward-stretching plateau of alluvium and ice.

The crushing, overthrusting and faulting that has affected the rocks of this system render it doubtful whether the coal seams which occur in it, even if of requisite thickness, can be worked to advantage. Some of the samples of coal obtained at the openings made near Yakutat bay were slickensided, showing that movements in the coal seam had there taken place.

As already stated, the rocks of the Yakutat series are remarkably uniform in character throughout the extent now known, and offer but little variety. The sandstones are intersected in every direction by thin quartz seams, which stand in relief on the weathered surfaces, giving the rocks a peculiar and characteristic appearance. The first important change in the geology along the route traversed by us was met on reaching Pinnacle pass.

PINNACLE SYSTEM.

The rocks of this system, as already stated, are best exposed in the great fault-scarp forming the northern wall of Pinnacle pass. They are more varied in composition and have preserved a better record of the conditions under which they were deposited than the sandstones and shales of the Yakutat system.

Only an approximate section of the rocks exposed in the Pinnacle-pass cliff was obtained.

Sandstone and conglomerate weathering into spires .	500 feet.
Evenly bedded, sandy shale in thin layers .	600 "
Coarse conglomerate ; bowlders of crystalline rock .	50 "
Thinly bedded, dark-colored sandstone and shale	500 "
Reddish conglomerate	10 "
Light-gray sandstone, with thin, irregular coal seams	40 "
Total	1,800 "

There is also a compact, crystalline, gray limestone near the upper portion of the series, which escaped notice in the cliffs. At the end of the Pinnacle-pass cliffs, however, where the rocks are turned northward by the great fault which decides the course of the Seward glacier, and dip eastward at a high angle, the limestone is well exposed, and has a thickness of about 50 feet. In many places the surfaces of the layers are covered with fragments of large *Pecten* shells. Associated with the limestone there are reddish shales, much crushed and broken, and a peculiar conglomerate. The pebbles in the conglomerate are of many varieties, and were observed at places along the Pinnacle pass cliffs. Their most marked peculiarity lies in the fact that they have been sheared by a movement in the rocks and sometimes broken into several fragments which have been reunited, probably by pressure. These faulted pebbles are characteristic of the strata from which they were derived. Similar pebbles were afterward obtained in the Marvine glacier near its junction with the Malaspina glacier, thus indicating that there are other outcrops of the conglomerate about Mount Cook, near where the Marvine glacier has its source. Two quartz pebbles from the conglomerate of Pinnacle pass are shown in the accompanying illustrations. The larger pebble (shown in figure 7) is of bluish-gray quartz, and the smaller one (depicted in figure 8) is of white quartz. The fragments into which they have been broken are now firmly united. The engravings are photo-mechanical (Moss process) reproductions from the objects.

In the northern and western part of the Samovar hills the rocks of the Pinnacle system again appear, forming a bold angular ridge, curving southward and reaching the border of the Agassiz glacier. The southern face of this range is precipitous and, like the Pinnacle pass cliffs, exhibits the edges of northward-dipping strata. Its northern and western slopes are heavily snowbound. It is in reality a continuation of the Pinnacle pass fault, but thrown out of line by the cross-fault which marked out the course of the Seward glacier.

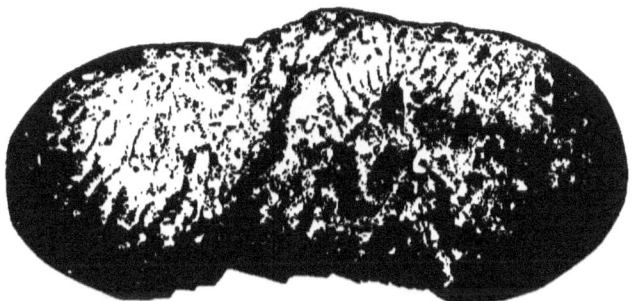

Figure 7.--*Faulted Pebble from Pinnacle Pass.*

The Yakutat and Pinnacle systems are so easily recognized that their distribution can be distinguished at a glance, when the outcrops are not concealed beneath the nearly universal covering of snow. The rocks of the Yakutat series are heavily bedded sandstones and shales, and have in general a light-brown tint; while the rocks of the Pinnacle series are thinly bedded and dark in color, appearing black at a distance.

The presence of a *Pecten* (*P. caurinus* (?) Gld.) in the limestone of the Pinnacle series has already been mentioned. Other fossils were obtained from sandstones and shales at the crest of the cliffs above Pinnacle pass at an elevation of 5,000 feet. These were submitted to Dr. W. H. Dall, who kindly identified them as follows:

Mya arenaria, L.;
Mytilus edulis, L.;
Leda fossa, Baird, or *L. minuta*, Fabr.:
Macoma inconspicua, B. and S.;
Cardium islandicum, L.;
Litorina atkana, Dall.

All of these species are stated by Dall to be still living in the oceanic waters of Alaska. The very recent age of the rocks in which they occur is thus established.

FIGURE 8—*Faulted Pebble from Pinnacle Pass.*

In strata closely connected with the layers in which these shells were found there occur many fine leaf impressions, a few of which were brought away. These have been examined by Professor L. F. Ward, who has identified them with four species of *Salix*, closely resembling living species. The report on these interesting fossils forms Appendix D.

The age indicated by both invertebrates and plants is late Tertiary (Pliocene) or early Pleistocene. This determination is of great significance when taken in connection with the structure of the region, and shows that the mountains in the St. Elias region are young.

Not only was a part, at least, of the Pinnacle system deposited during the life of living species of mollusks, but also the whole of the Yakutat series, the stratigraphic position of which is, if my determination is correct, above the Pinnacle system. After the sediments composing the rocks of these two series were de-

posited in the sea as strata of sand, mud, etc., they were consoli-
dated, overthrust, faulted, and upheaved into one of the grandest
mountain ridges on the continent. Then, after the mountains
had reached a considerable height, if not their full growth, the
snows of winter fell upon them, and glaciers were born; the
glaciers increased to a maximum, and their surfaces reached
from a thousand to two thousand feet higher than now on the
more southern mountain spurs, and afterward slowly wasted
away to their present dimensions. All of this interesting and
varied history has been enacted during the life of existing species
of plants and animals.

The relative age of the Yakutat and Pinnacle series is the
weakest point in the history sketched above. The facts on which
it rests are as follows: At Pinnacle pass the sandstones and
shales forming the southern wall belong to the Yakutat system
and are much disturbed, while the northern wall, or the heaved
side of the fault, is composed of the rocks of the Pinnacle system, inclined northward at an angle of 30° or 40°. North of
this fault-scarp, in the foothills of Mount Owen, sandstones and
shales, seemingly identical with those of the Yakutat system,
again occur, although their direct connection with the rocks
south of Pinnacle pass was not observed, owing to the snow that
obscured the outcrops. Again at Dome pass a similar relation
seems evident, but cannot be directly established. The immediate foothills of Mounts Augusta, Malaspina, and St. Elias are
also of sandstone, lithologically the same as the Yakutat series.
The conclusion that the Yakutat system is younger than the
Pinnacle-pass rocks was reached in the field after many other
hypotheses had been tried and found wanting, and to my mind
it explains all the observations made. Even should the supposed relations of the two series under discussion be reversed, it
would still be true that a very large part of the rocks of the St.
Elias region were deposited since the appearance of living species
of mollusks and plants, and that the prevailing structure of the
region was imposed at a still later date. This will appear more
clearly after examining the structure of the region.

St. Elias Schist.

The rock forming several thousand feet of the upper portion
of the St. Elias range is a schist in which the planes of bedding

are preserved. The dip of the strata is northeastward, and has exerted a decided influence on the weathering of the mountain crests. As the opportunities for examining this formation were unsatisfactory, a detailed account of it will not now be attempted.

GEOLOGICAL STRUCTURE.

The abnormal thickness of the Yakutat series, due to crushing and overthrust, has been referred to, as has also the superposition of the St. Elias schist upon rock supposed to belong to the Yakutat system.

The plane of contact between the sandstone and the overlying schist of the St. Elias range dips northeastward at an angle of about 15°, corresponding, as nearly as can be determined, with the dip of the strata in the sandstone itself. All of the observations made in this connection indicate that the schist has been overthrust upon the sandstones. After this took place the great faults to which the range owes its present relief were formed.

About Mount Cook, however, and in the elevated plateau east of Yakutat bay, the conditions are different from those observed along the base of the St. Elias range. The only displacements known in the Yakutat system south and east of Pinnacle pass is the great fault which presumably exists where the rocks of the foothills disappear beneath the gravel and glaciers of the Piedmont region, the faults referred to belonging to the same series as those which determine the southern and southwestern borders of the St. Elias range and many of the foothills south of the main escarpment. Besides the great faults which trend from St. Elias toward the northeast and northwest, there are several cross-faults, one of which determines the position of the Seward glacier through a portion of its course, while another marks out the path of the Agassiz glacier; and two others may be recognized just east of the summit of St. Elias, which have dropped portions of the eastern end of the orographic block forming the crowning peak of the range.

The southern face of Mount St. Elias is a fault-scarp. The mountain itself is formed by the upturned edge of a faulted block in which the stratification is inclined northeastward. As has just been mentioned, the mountain stands at the intersection of two lines of displacement, one trending in a northeasterly and the other in a northwesterly direction. The one trending northwestward extends beyond the end of the northeast fault. The point of union is at the pass between Mount St. Elias and Mount Newton. The upturned block, bounded on the southwest by a great fault, projects beyond the junction with the northeasterly fault. It is this projecting end of a roof-like block that forms Mount St. Elias. That this is the case may be clearly seen when viewing the mountain from the glacier near the base of Mount Owen. Such a view is shown on plate 20. The crest-line of St. Elias extends with a decreasing grade northwestward from the culminating peak, and the northern slope of the ridge is the surface of the tilted block.

From what has been stated already, it will be seen that the St. Elias range is young. Its upheaval, as indicated by our present knowledge, was since the close of the Tertiary. The breaking of the rocks and their upheaval is an event of such recent date that erosion has scarcely modified the forms which the mountains had at their birth. The formation of glaciers followed the elevation of the region so quickly that there was no opportunity for streams to act. The ice drainage is consequent upon the geological structure, and has made but slight changes in the topography due to that structure.

About Mount Cook, and in the elevated plateau east of Yakutat bay, there has been deeper erosion than about Mount St. Elias. The glaciers in this region occupy deep valleys radiating from the higher peaks; but whether these are really valleys of erosion is not definitely known. In some instances, changes of dip on opposite sides of the valleys indicate that they may in part be due to faulting; but, owing principally to the fact that every basin has its glacier, it has not been practicable, up to the present time, to determine how they were formed.

The crests of the mountains are always sharp and angular, by reason of the rapid weathering of their exposed summits, but while disintegration is rapid, no evidences of pronounced decay are noticeable. The peaks on the summits of the St. Elias range are either pyramids or roof-like crests with triangular gables. These forms have resulted from the weathering of schist in which the planes of bedding are crossed by lines of jointing.

PART IV

GLACIERS OF THE ST. ELIAS REGION.

NATURAL DIVISIONS OF GLACIERS.

The glaciers of the St. Elias region form two groups. The ice-streams from the mountain are of the type found in Switzerland, and hence termed *Alpine glaciers*. The great plateau of ice along the ocean formed by the union and expansion of Alpine glaciers from the mountains belongs to a class not previously described, but which in this paper have been called *Piedmont glaciers*. The representative of the latter type between Yakutat bay and Icy bay is the Malaspina glacier. Both types are to be distinguished from *Continental glaciers*.

ALPINE GLACIERS.

The glaciers in the mountains are all of one type, but present great diversity in their secondary features, and might be separated into three or four subordinate divisions. The great trunk glaciers have many tributaries, and drain the snows from the mountains through broad channels, which are of low grade throughout all the lower portions of their courses. Besides the trunk glaciers and the secondary glaciers which flow into them, there are many smaller glaciers which do not join the main streams, but terminate in the gorges or on the exposed mountain sides in which they originate. These have nearly all the features of the larger streams, but are not of sufficient volume to become rivers of ice.

A minor division of Alpine glaciers for which it is convenient to have a special name includes those that end in the sea and, breaking off, form icebergs. These may be designated as "tidewater glaciers." Typical examples of this class are furnished by the Dalton and Hubbard glaciers, but other ice-streams having the same characteristics occur in Glacier bay, in Taku inlet, and at the heads of several of the deep fjords along the coast of southeastern Alaska.

(176)

A noticeable feature of the Alpine glaciers of Alaska is that they expand on passing beyond the valleys through which they flow and form delta-like accumulations of ice on the plains below. This expansion takes place irrespective of the direction in which the glaciers flow, and, so far as may be judged from the many examples examined, is independent of the débris that covers them. It should be remembered, however, that none of the Alaskan glaciers thus far studied show marked inequalities in the distribution of the moraines upon their surfaces. Should one side of a glacier, on leaving a cañon, be heavily loaded with marginal moraines, while the opposite border was unprotected, it is to be presumed that a deflection of the ice would take place similar to the change in direction recorded by the moraines about Mono lake, California.* The normal tendency of ice, when not confined, to expand in all directions and form a plateau is illustrated on a grand scale by the Malaspina glacier.

The most important ice-streams about Mount St. Elias and Mount Cook are indicated on the map forming plate 8. The Tindall, Guyot, and Libbey glaciers and the lower part of the Agassiz glacier there represented are taken from a map published by H. W. Topham.† All of the other glaciers indicated on the map were hastily surveyed during the present expedition and are described to some extent in the accompanying narrative. By far the most important of these is the one named the Seward Glacier.

The Seward Glacier is of the Alpine type, and is the largest tributary of the Malaspina glacier. Its length is approximately 10 miles, and its width in the narrowest part, opposite Camp fourteen, is about 3 miles. The main amphitheatre from which its drainage is derived is north of Mount Owen and between Mount Irving and Mount Logan. The general surface of the broad level floor of this névé field has an elevation of approximately 5,000 feet. The snow from the northern and western sides of Mount Irving, from the northern slope of Mount Owen, and from numerous valleys and cañons in the vast semicircle of towering peaks joining these two mountains, unite to form the great glacier. There is another amphitheatre between Mount Owen and the Pinnacle pass cliffs supplied principally by snows

* Eighth Ann. Rept. U. S. Geol. Surv., 1889, part I, pp. 360–366.
† Alpine Journal, London, vol. XIV, 1887, pl. op. p. 359.

from the northwestern slope of Mount Cook, which sends a vast flood of ice and snow into the main drainage channel. Other tributary glaciers descend the steep slopes of Mount Augusta and Mount Malaspina, and a lesser tributary flows eastward from Dome pass. All of these ice-drainage lines converge toward the narrow outlet of Camp 14 (plate 8) and discharge southward down a moderately steep descent several miles in length. Below Camp 14 there are other névé fields bordering the glacier, which contribute no insignificant amount of ice and snow to its mass. Between the extremity of the Hitchcock range and the Samovar hills the path of the glacier is again contracted and greatly broken as it descends to the plateau below.

The Seward glacier, like all ice rivers of its class, has its névé region above, and its ice region below. The limit between the two is the lower margin of the summer snow, and occurs just above the ice-fall between the southern extremity of the Hitchcock range and the Samovar hills. All the névé region is pure white and without moraines, except at the immediate bases of the most precipitous cliffs. At the bases of the Corwin cliffs, which rise fully 2,000 feet above its border, no débris can be distinguished even in midsummer. An absence of moraines along the base of Pinnacle pass cliffs was also noticed during our first visit, but when we returned over the same route in September the melting of the snow had revealed many large patches of dirt and disintegrated rock. In several places near the bases of steep cliffs, strata of dirty ice, containing many stones, were observed in deep crevasses. It was evident that vast quantities of débris were sealed up in the ice along the borders of the glacier, only to appear at the surface far down the stream where summer melting exceeds the winter accumulation.

The surface of the glacier below the lower fall is composed of solid ice with blue and white bands, and has broad moraines along its borders. The course of the glacier, after entering the great plateau of ice to which it is tributary, may be traced for many miles by the bands of débris along its sides. These moraines belong to the Malaspina glacier, and have already been referred to.

At the outlet of the upper amphitheatre, about 6 miles above Mount Owen, there is an ice-fall which extends completely across the glacier. Below the pinnacles and crevasses formed by this fall the ice is recemented and flows on with a broad, gently descending surface, gashed, however, by thousands of crevasses, as shown in plate 20, to the end of the Pinnacle pass cliffs. It there finds a more rapid descent, and becomes crevassed in an interesting way. The slope is not sufficient to be termed a fall, but causes a rapid in the ice-stream.

The change of grade in the bed of the glacier is first felt about a mile above Camp 14. A series of crevasses there begins, which extends four or five miles down-stream. At first the cracks are narrow, and trend upstream in the manner usual with marginal crevasses. Soon the cracks from the opposite sides meet in the center and form a single crevasse, bending upstream in the middle. A little lower down, the crevasse becomes straight, showing that the ice in the center of the current flows more rapidly than at the sides. The more rapid movement of the center is indicated by the form of the crevasses all the way down the rapid. After becoming straight they bow in the center and form semi-lunar gashes, widest in the center and curving up-stream at each extremity. Still farther down they become more and more bent in the center and at the same time greatly increased in breadth. Still lower the curve becomes an angle and the crevasses are V-shaped, the arrow-like point directed down-stream. These parallel V-shaped gashes set in order, one in front of the other, are what gives the glacier the appearance of "watered" ribbon when seen from a distance.

With the change in direction and curvature of the crevasses, there is an accompanying change in color. The cracks in the upper part of the rapid are in a white surface and run down into ice that looks dark and blue by contrast. Lower down, as the cracks increase in width, broad white tables are left between them. Cross-fractures are formed, and the sides of the table begin to crumble in and fill up the gaps between. As the surface melts the tables lose their pure whiteness and become dust-covered and yellow; but the blocks falling into the crevasses expose fresh surfaces, and fill the gulfs with pure white ice. In this way the color of the sides of the crevasses changes from deep blue to white, while the general surface loses its purity and becomes dust-covered. Far down the rapid where the V-shaped crevasses are most pointed, the tables have crumbled away and filled up the gulfs between, so that the watered-ribbon pattern is distinguished by color alone. The scars of the crevasses formed above are shown by white bands on a dark dust-covered surface. Before the lower fall is reached nearly all traces of the thousands of fissures formed in the rapids above have disappeared.

On looking down on the rapids from any commanding point, the definite arrangement of the crevasses along the center of the ice-stream at once attracts attention, and their order suggests a rapid central current in the stream.

Below Camp 14, for at least two or three miles, as well as at many places above that point, the Seward glacier flows between banks of snow. Along its border there are marginal crevasses trending up-stream, and in the adjacent banks there are similar breaks trending down-stream. Where the two systems meet there is a line of irregular crevasses, exceedingly difficult to cross, which mark the actual border of the flowing ice. A similar arrangement of marginal crevasses and of shore crevasses has been referred to in connection with the Marvine glacier, and was observed in many other instances.

While occupying Camp 14 we could hear the murmur of waters far down in the glacier below our tent, but there were no surface streams visible. Crashing and rumbling noises made by the slowly moving ice frequently attracted our attention, and sometimes at night we would be awakened by a dull thud, accompanied by a trembling of the rocks beneath us, as if a slight earthquake had occurred. Occasionally a pinnacle of ice would fall and be engulfed in the crevasses at its base. These evidences of change indicated that movements in the Seward glacier were constantly in progress. A short base-line was measured and sights taken to well-marked points in the Seward glacier for the purpose of measuring its motion. The angles between the base-line and lines of sight to the chosen points were read on several successive days, but when these observations were compared they gave discrepant results. The measurements which seemed most reliable indicate that the central part of the ice-stream has a movement of about twenty feet a day. This is to be taken only as an approximation, which needs to be verified before much weight can be attached to it.

CHARACTERISTICS OF ALPINE GLACIERS ABOVE THE SNOW-LINE.

The surface of the névé is white, except near its lower limit in late summer, where it frequently becomes covered with dust blown from neighboring cliffs. It is almost entirely free from moraines, but at the bases of steep slopes small areas of débris sometimes appear at the surface when the yearly melting has reached its maximum. The absence of moraines is accompanied by an absence of glacial tables, sand-cones and other details of glacial surfaces due to differential melting. Streams seldom appear at the surface, for the reason that usually the water produced by surface melting is quickly absorbed by the porous strata beneath ; yet the crevasses are frequently filled with water, and sometimes shallow lakes of deep blue occur at the bottoms of the amphitheatres and form a marked contrast to the even white of the general surface. Crevasses are present or absent according to the slope of the surface on which the névé rests. In the crevasses the edges of horizontal layers of granular ice are exhibited, showing that the névé down to a depth of at least one or two hundred feet is horizontally stratified. In the St. Elias region the strata are most frequently from ten to fifteen feet thick, but in a few instances layers without partings over fifty feet thick were seen. The surface is always of white, granular ice, but in the crevasses the layers near the bottom appear more compact and bluer in color than those near the surface.

Some of the most striking features of the névé are due to the crevasses that break their surfaces. The orderly arrangement of marginal crevasses and of the interior crevasses at the rapids in the Seward glacier have already been referred to; but there are still other crevasses, especially in the broad, gently sloping portions of the snow-fields where the motion is slight, which, although less regular in their arrangement, are fully as interesting. The crevasses on such slopes generally run at right angles to the direction in which the snow is moving. On looking down on such a surface, the breaks look like long clear-cut gashes which have stretched open in the center, but taper to a sharp point at each end. The ability of the névé ice to stretch to a limited extent is thus clearly shown. The initiation of the crevasses seems to be due to the movement of the névé ice over a surface in which there are inequalities of such magnitude that the ice cannot stretch sufficiently to allow it to accommodate itself to them, so that strains are produced which result in fractures at right angles to the line of general movement. Crevasses found where the grade is gentle vary from a fraction of an inch to 10 or 15 feet in width, and are sometimes two or three thousand feet long. Broader gulfs are seldom formed unless the slope has an inclination of 15° or 20°.

The grandest crevasses are in the higher portions of the névé, and occur especially on the borders of the great amphitheatres. In such situations the crevasses are usually fewer in number but are of greater size than in equal areas lower down. A length of three or four thousand feet and a breadth of fifty feet or more is not uncommon. The finest and most characteristic glacial scenery is found among these great cañon-like breaks. Standing on the border of one of the gulfs, as near the brink as one cares to venture, their full depth cannot usually be seen. In some instances they are partially filled with water of the deepest blue, in which the ice-walls are reflected with such wonderful distinctness that it is impossible to tell where the ice ends and its counterfeit begins. The walls of the crevasses are most frequently sheer cliffs of stratified ice, with occasional ornamentations, formed of ice-crystals or a pendent icicle. After a storm they are frequently decorated in the most beautiful manner with fretwork and cornice of snow. The bridges spanning the crevasses are usually diagonal slivers of ice left where the clefts overlap; but at times, especially in the case of the larger crevasses, there are true arches resembling the Natural Bridge of Virginia, but on a larger scale, spanning the blue cañons and adding greatly to their strange, fairy-like beauty. The most striking feature of these cracks is their wonderful color. All tints, from the pure white of their crystal lips down to the deepest blue of their innermost recesses, are revealed in each gash and rent in the hardened snow.

Above the snow-line all of the mountain tops that are not precipitous are heavily loaded with snow. Where the snow breaks off at the verge of a precipice and descends in avalanches a depth of more than a hundred feet is frequently revealed, but in the valleys and amphitheatres the snow has far greater thickness. Pinnacles and crests of rock, rising through the icy covering, indicate that the thickness of the névé must be many hundreds of feet.

There are no evidences of former glaciation on the mountain crests which project above the névé fields. There are no polished and striated rock surfaces or glaciated domes to indicate that the mountains were ever covered by a general capping of ice, as has been postulated for similar mountains elsewhere. When the glaciers had their greatest expansion the higher mountains were in about their present condition. The increase in the volume of the glaciers was felt almost entirely in their lower courses.

CHARACTERISTICS OF ALPINE GLACIERS BELOW THE SNOW-LINE.

The first feature that attracts attention on descending from the névé region to the more icy portion of the glaciers is the rapid melting everywhere taking place. Every day during the summer the murmur and roar of rills, brooks and rivers are to be heard in all of the ice-fields. The surface streams are usually short, on account of the crevasses which intercept them. They plunge into the gulfs, which are many times widened out by the flowing waters so as to form wells, or *moulins*, and join the general drainage beneath. The streams then flow either through caverns in the glaciers or in tunnels at the bottoms. While traversing the glacier one may frequently hear the subdued roar of rivers coursing along in the dark chambers beneath when no other indication of their existence appears at the surface. When these subglacial streams emerge, usually near the margin of the ice, they issue from archways forming the ends of tunnels, and perhaps flow for a mile or two in the sunlight before plunging into another tunnel to continue their way as before.

The best example of a glacial river seen during our exploration was near the western border of the Lucia glacier. It is shown in the illustration forming plate 12, which is reproduced mechanically from a photograph. This Styx of the ice-world has been described on an earlier page. The lakes formed at the southern end of nearly every mountain spur projecting into the Malaspina glacier discharge through tunnels in the ice, which are similar in every way to those formed by the stream already mentioned.

In the beds of the glacial streams there are deposits of sand and gravel, and when the streams expand into lakes these deposits are spread over their bottoms in more or less regular sheets. When streams from the mountains empty into the lakes, deltas are formed. While these deltas have the same characteristics as those built in more stable water bodies, many changes in detail occur, owing to the fluctuation of the water level.

One of the tunnels leading to a dry lake-bed at the end of the Hitchcock range was explored for several rods and found to be a high, arching cavern following a tortuous course, and large enough to allow one to drive a coach and four through it without danger of collision. Its floor was formed of gravel and bowlders, and its arching roof was clear ice. Here and there the courses of crevasses could be traced by the stones and finer débris that had fallen in from above, giving the appearance of veins in a mine. The deposit on the floor of the tunnel rested upon ice, and would certainly be greatly disturbed and broken up before reaching a final resting place in case the glacier should melt. In the lake basins, also, the sand and gravel forming their bottoms frequently rested upon substrata of ice, and are greatly disturbed when the ice melts.

At the ends of the glaciers the subglacial and intraglacial drainage issues from tunnels and forms muddy streams. These usually flow out from the foot of a precipice of ice, down which rills are continually trickling. The streams flowing away from the glaciers are usually rapid, owing to the high grade of their built-up channels, and sweep away large quantities of débris which is deposited along their courses. The streams widen and bifurcate as they flow seaward, and spread vast quantities of bowlders, sand, and gravel over the country to the right and left, not infrequently invading the forests and burying the still upright trees. The deposits formed by the streams are of the nature of alluvial fans, over which the waters meander in a thousand channels. Where this action has taken place long enough the alluvial fans end in deltas; but should there be a current in the sea, the débris is carried away and formed into beaches and bars along adjacent shores. Should these glaciers disappear, it is evident that these great bowlder washes would form peculiar topographic features, unsupported at the apexes, and it might be perplexing to determine from whence came the waters that deposited them. I am not aware that similar washes have been recognized along the southern border of the Laurentide glaciers, but they should certainly be expected to occur there.

Another very striking difference in the appearance of the glaciers above and below the snow-line is due to the prevalence of débris on the lower portion. The melting that takes place below the snow-line removes the ice and leaves the rocks. In this manner the stones previously concealed in the névé are concentrated at the surface, and finally form sheets of débris many miles in extent. So far as my observations go, there is nothing to indicate that stones are brought to the surface by any other means than the one here suggested. Upward currents in the ice that would bring stones to the surface have been postulated by certain writers, but nothing sustaining such an hypothesis has been found in Alaska.

The moraines on the lower extremities of the Alpine glaciers may frequently be separated into individual ridges, which in many instances would furnish instructive studies; but in no case has the history of these accumulations been worked out in detail.

With the appearance of moraines at the surface come a great variety of phenomena due to unequal melting. Ridges of ice sheathed with débris, glacial tables, sand cones, etc., everywhere attract the attention; but these features are very similar on all glaciers where the summer's waste exceeds the winter's increase, and have been many times described.

The general distribution of the moraines of the lower portion of the Alpine glaciers of the St. Elias region merits attention. The moraines themselves exhibit features not yet observed in other regions. From Disenchantment bay westward to the Seward glacier the lower portions of the ice-streams are covered and concealed by sheets of débris. About their margins the débris fields support luxuriant vegetation, and not infrequently are so densely clothed with flowers that a tint is given to their rugged surfaces. On the extreme outer margins of the moraines there are sometimes thickets and forests so dense as to be almost impenetrable. The best example of forest-covered moraines resting on living glaciers, however, is found along the borders of the Malaspina ice-field.

PIEDMONT GLACIERS.

This type is represented in the region explored by the Malaspina glacier. This is a plateau of ice having an area of between 500 and 600 square miles, and a surface elevation in the central part of between 1,500 and 1,600 feet. It is fed by the Agassiz, Seward, Marvine, and Hayden glaciers, and is of such volume that it has apparently displaced the sea and holds it back by a wall of débris deposited about its margin. All of its central portion is of clear white ice, and around all its margins, excepting where the Agassiz and Seward glaciers come in, it is bounded by a fringe of débris and by moraines resting on the ice. Along the seaward border the belt of fringing moraines is about five miles broad. The inner margin of the moraine belt is composed of rocks and dirt, without vegetation, and separated more or less completely into belts by strips of clear ice. On going from the clear ice toward the margin of the glacier one finds shrubs and flowers scattered here and there over the surface. Farther seaward the vegetation becomes more dense and the flowers cover the whole surface, giving it the appearance of a luxuriant meadow. Still farther toward the margin dense clumps of alder, with scattered spruce trees, become conspicuous, while on the outer margin spruce trees of larger size form a veritable forest. That this vegetation actually grows on the moraines above a living glacier is proved beyond all question by holes and crevasses which reveal the ice beneath. The curious lakes scattered abundantly over the moraine-covered areas, and occupying hour-glass-shaped depressions in the ice, have already been described.

From the southern end of the Samovar hills, where the Seward and Agassiz glaciers unite, there is a compound moraine stretching southward, which divides at its distal extremity and forms great curves and swirl-like figures indicating currents in the glacier.

All the central part of the plateau is, as already stated, of clear white ice, free from moraines; at a distance it has the appearance of a broad snow surface. This is due to the fact that the ice is melted and honey-combed during the warm summer and the surface becomes vesicular and loses its banded structure. A rough, coral-like crust, due to the freezing of the portions melted during the day, frequently covers large areas and resembles a thick hoar-frost. Crevasses are numerous, but seldom more than a few feet deep. They appear to be the lower portions of deep crevasses in the tributary streams which have partially closed, or else not completely removed by the melting and evaporation of the surface.

Many of the crevasses are filled with water, but there are no surface streams and no lakes. Melting is rapid during the warm summer days, but the water finds its way down into the glacier and joins the general subglacial drainage. It is evident that the streams beneath the surface must be of large size, as they furnish the only means of escape for the waters flowing beneath the Agassiz, Seward and Marvine glaciers, as well as for the waters formed by the melting of the great Malaspina glacier.

The outer borders of the Malaspina glacier are practically stationary, but there are currents in its central part. Like the expanded ends of some of the Alpine glaciers, as the Galiano and Lucia glaciers, for example, this glacier is of the nature of a delta of ice, analogous in many of its features to river deltas. As a stream in meandering over its delta builds up one portion after another, so the currents in an expanded ice-foot may now follow one direction and deposit loads of débris, and then slowly change so as to occupy other positions. This action tends to destroy the individuality of morainal belts and to form general sheets of débris. The presence of such currents as here suggested has not been proved by measurements, but the great swirls in the Malaspina glacier and the tongues of clear ice in the upper portions of the débris fields on the smaller glaciers strongly suggest their existence.

The Malaspina glacier is evidently not eroding its bed; any records that it is making must be by deposition. Should the glacier melt away completely, it is evident that a surface formed of glacial débris, and very similar to that now existing in the forested plateau east of Yakutat bay, would be revealed.

The former extent of the Malaspina glacier cannot be determined, but it is probable that during its greatest expansion it extended seaward until deep water was reached, and broke off in bergs in the same manner as do the Greenland glaciers at the present day. Soundings in the adjacent waters might possibly determine approximately the former position of the ice-front, and it is possible that submarine moraines might be discovered in this way. The Pimpluna reefs, reported by Russian navigators and indicated on many maps, may possibly be a remnant of the moraine left by the Piedmont glacier from the adjacent coast.

The glaciers west of Icy bay were seen from the top of Pinnacle pass cliffs, and are evidently of the same character as the Malaspina glacier and fully as extensive. A study of these Pied-

mont glaciers will certainly throw much light on the interpreta-
tions of the glacial records over northeastern North America.
Their value in this connection is enhanced by the fact that they
are now retreating and making deposits rather than removing
previous geological records.

The expedition of last summer was a hasty reconnoissance,
during which but little detail work could be undertaken. The
actual study of the ice-fields of the St. Elias region remains for
those who come later.

PART V

HEIGHT AND POSITION OF MOUNT ST. ELIAS.

The height and position of Mount St. Elias have been measured several times during the past century with varying results. The measurements made prior to the expedition of 1890 have been summarized and discussed by W. H. Dall, of the United States Coast and Geodetic Survey, and little more can be done at present than give an abstract of his report.

The various determinations are shown in the table below. The data from which these results were obtained have not been published, with the exception of the surveys made by the United States Coast Survey in 1874, printed in report of the superintendent for 1875.

Height and Position of Mount St. Elias.

Date.	Authority.	Height.	Latitude.	Longitude W.
1786	La Pérouse	12,672 feet	60° 15′ 00″	140° 10′ 00″
1791	Malaspina	17,851 "	60 17 35	140 52 17
1794	Vancouver		60 22 30	140 39 00
1847	Russian Hydrographic Chart 1378	17,854 "	60 21 00	141 00 00
1847	Tebenkof (Notes)	16,938 "	60 22 36	140 54 00
1849	Tebenkof (Chart VII)	16,938 "	60 21 30	140 54 00
	Buch, Can. Inseln	16,758 "	60 17 30	140 51 00
1872	English Admiralty Chart 2172	14,970 "	60 21 00	141 00 00
1874	U. S. Coast Survey	19,500±400	60 20 45	141 00 12

All of the figures given in the table have been copied from Dall's report, with the exception of the position determined by Malaspina; this is from a report of astronomical observations made during Malaspina's voyage, which places the mountain in latitude 60° 17′ 35″ and longitude 131° 33′ 10″ west of Cadiz.[*] Taking the longitude of Cadiz as 6° 19′ 07″ west of Greenwich, the figures tabulated above are obtained.

[*] Ante, p. 65.

It was intended that Mr. Kerr's report, forming Appendix B, should contain a detailed record of the triangulation executed last summer, but a careful revision of his work by a committee of the National Geographic Society led to the conclusion that the results were not of sufficient accuracy to set at rest the questions raised by the discrepancies in earlier measurements of the height of Mount St. Elias; and as the work will probably be revised and extended during the summer of 1891, only the map forming plate 8 will be published at this time. Some preliminary publications of elevations have been made, but these must be taken as approximations merely.*

By consulting the map forming plate 8 it will be seen that Mounts Cook, Vancouver, Irving, Owen, etc., are not in the St. Elias range. Neither do they form a distinct range either topographically or geologically. Each of these mountains is an independent uplift, although they may have some structural connection, and are of about the same geological age. Mount Cook and the peaks most intimately associated with it are composed mainly of sandstone and shale belonging to the Yakutat system. Mounts Vancouver and Irving are probably of the same character, but definite proof that this is the case has not been obtained.

The St. Elias uplift is distinct and well marked, both geologically and topographically, and deserves to be considered as a mountain range. The limits of the range have not been determined, but, so far as known, its maximum elevation is at Mount St. Elias. The range stretches away from this culminating point both northeastward and northwestward, and has a well-marked V-shape. The angle formed by the two branches of the range where they unite at Mount St. Elias is, by estimate, about 140°. Each arm of the V is determined by a fault, or perhaps more accurately by a series of faults having the same general course, along which the orographic blocks forming the range have been upheaved. The structure of the range is monoclinal, and re-

* The shore-line of the map, plate 8, and the positions of the initial points or base-line of the triangulation are from the work of the United States Coast Survey. The extreme western portion is from maps published by the New York *Times* and Topham expeditions. All the topographic data are by Mr. Kerr, and all credit for the work and all responsibility for its accuracy rest with him. The nomenclature is principally my own, and has been approved by a committee of the National Geographic Society.

MT ST ELIAS, FROM THE SEWARD GLACIER.

sembles the type of mountain structure characteristic of the great basin. The dip of the tilted blocks is northward.

The crest of the St. Elias range, as already stated, is composed of schists which rest on sandstone, supposed to belong to the Yakutat system. The geological age of the uplift is, therefore, very recent. The secondary topographic forms on the crest of the range have resulted from the weathering of the upturned edges of orographic blocks in which the bedding planes are crossed by joints. The resulting forms are mainly pyramids and roof-like ridges with triangular gables. Extreme ruggedness and angularity characterize the range throughout. There are no rounded domes or smoothed and polished surfaces to suggest that the higher summits have ever been subjected to general glacial action; neither is there any evidence of marked rock decay. Disintegration of all the higher peaks and crests is rapid, owing principally to great changes of temperature and the freezing of water in the interstices of the rock; but the débris resulting from this action is rapidly carried away by avalanches and glaciers, so that the crests as well as the subordinate features in the sculpture of the cliffs and pyramids are all angular. The subdued and rounded contour, due to the accumulation of the products of disintegration and decay, the indications of the advancing age of mountains, are nowhere to be seen. The St. Elias range is young; probably the very youngest of the important mountain ranges on this continent. No evidences of erosion previous to the formation of the ice-sheets that now clothe it have been observed. Glaciers apparently took immediate possession of the lines of depression as the mountain range grew in height, and furnish a living example from which to determine the part that ice streams play in mountain sculpture.

Appendix A.

OFFICIAL INSTRUCTIONS GOVERNING THE EXPEDITION.

In order to make the records of the St. Elias expedition complete, copies of the instructions under which the work was carried out are appended:

DEPARTMENT OF THE INTERIOR,
UNITED STATES GEOLOGICAL SURVEY, GEOLOGIC BRANCH,
Washington, D. C., May 28, 1890.

Mr. I. C. RUSSELL, *Geologist.*

SIR: You are hereby detailed to visit the St. Elias range of Alaska for work of exploration, under the joint auspices of the National Geographic Society and the United States Geological Survey. The Geological Survey furnishes instruments and contributes the sum of $1,000 towards the expenses of the expedition. The money devoted to this purpose is taken from the appropriation for the fiscal year ending June 30, 1890, and the manner of its expenditure must conform to that fact.

The Survey expects that you will give special attention to glaciers, to their distribution, to the associated topographic types, to indications of the former extent of glaciation, and to types of subaërial sculpture under special conditions of erosion, and that you will also bring back information with reference to the age of the formations seen and the type of structure of the range.

With the aid of Mr. Kerr, it is expected that you will secure definite geographic information as to the belt of country traversed by you.

Very respectfully,   G. K. GILBERT,
Chief Geologist.

Approved,
J. W. POWELL, *Director.*

———

DEPARTMENT OF THE INTERIOR,
UNITED STATES GEOLOGICAL SURVEY, GEOLOGIC BRANCH.
Washington, D. C., May 28, 1890.

Mr. I. C. RUSSELL, *Geologist.*

SIR: You will proceed at the earliest practicable date to Tacoma, Washington Territory, and thence by water to Sitka, Alaska, at which point you will make special arrangements to visit the St. Elias range of mountains and make geological examinations as per instructions otherwise communicated. Mr. Mark B. Kerr, Disbursing Agent, will report to you at Victoria, B. C., and accompany you on the expedition, assisting you in the capacities of Disbursing Agent and Topographer. On the completion of

(192)

your work you will return to Washington, the route being left to your discretion, to be determined by considerations which cannot now be foreseen.

Very respectfully, G. K. GILBERT,
Chief Geologist.

Approved,
J. W. POWELL, *Director.*

———

DEPARTMENT OF THE INTERIOR,
UNITED STATES GEOLOGICAL SURVEY, GEOLOGIC BRANCH,
Washington, D. C., May 28, 1890.

Mr. MARK B. KERR, *Disbursing Agent.*

SIR: You are hereby detailed to assist Mr. I. C. Russell, Geologist, who starts at once on an expedition to Alaska, under the joint auspices of the National Geographic Society and the United States Geological Survey. It is expected that you will immediately aid him in disbursement, and that you will act during the exploratory part of the expedition as topographer. Your duties will, however, not be limited to these special functions, but you will be expected to perform any other duties he may assign to you, and to labor in every way for the success of the expedition.

It is expected that you will be reappointed to the grade of topographer on the United States Geological Survey on the 1st of July, 1890, and you will please take the required oath of office before your departure.

The money remaining in your possession as Disbursing Agent includes that needed to meet Mr. Russell's salary and your own, and also the sum of $1,000, allotted from the funds of the Geographic Branch for expenses of the expedition prior to June 30. This amount you will expend as directed by Mr. Russell, and his authority and certificate will need to accompany your vouchers in rendering account of the same.

Very respectfully, G. K. GILBERT,
Chief Geologist.

Approved,
J. W. POWELL, *Director.*

———

DEPARTMENT OF THE INTERIOR,
UNITED STATES GEOLOGICAL SURVEY, GEOLOGIC BRANCH,
Washington, D. C., May 28, 1890.

Mr. MARK B. KERR,
Disbursing Agent.

SIR: You will proceed at once to San Francisco, California, and thence by steamer or by rail and steamer to Sitka, Alaska. It is expected that you will join Mr. I. C. Russell, Geologist, at Victoria, B. C., or at Sitka ; and you will report to him for further orders.

Very respectfully, G. K. GILBERT,
Chief Geologist.

Approved,
J. W. POWELL, *Director.*

Washington, D. C., May 29, 1890.

Mr. MARK B. KERR, *Topographer.*

SIR: You are hereby assigned to field-work in the vicinity of Mount St. Elias, Alaska, in the party under charge of Mr. I. C. Russell. Upon the receipt of these instructions you will please proceed without delay to the field, and map upon a scale of four miles to an inch such territory in the vicinity of Mount St. Elias, including that mountain, as the field season will permit. The work should, if practicable, be controlled by triangulation. Special attention in the course of your work should be given to measuring the altitude of Mount St. Elias, and it should be determined by triangulation and also, if practicable, by barometer in such manner as to be conclusive.

The topographic work should be controlled by triangulation. As many positions on this coast are approximately known, including a number of the prominent peaks, astronomical determinations of position will not be necessary unless needed to supplement the triangulation.

The details of your outfitting and the management of the work will be left to your own judgment.

Very respectfully,

HENRY GANNETT,
Chief Topographer.

NATIONAL GEOGRAPHIC SOCIETY.

Memorandum of Instructions to the Party sent out under the Direction of Mr. I. C. Russell, assisted by Mr. Mark B. Kerr, to explore the Mount St. Elias Region, Alaska, 1890.

The general object of the expedition is to make a geographic reconnoissance of as large an area as practicable in the St. Elias range, Alaska, including a study of its glacial phenomena, the preparation of a map of the region explored, and the measurement of the height of Mount St. Elias and other neighboring mountains. Observations should also be made and information collected on other subjects of general scientific interest as far as practicable.

The purpose of these instructions is mainly to suggest the lines of investigation that give promise of valuable results, but it is not intended that they shall limit the director of the expedition in the exercise of his own discretion.

GARDINER G. HUBBARD, *Chairman,*
MARCUS BAKER,
WILLARD D. JOHNSON,
Committee.

Washington, D. C., May 29, 1890.

Appendix B.

REPORT ON TOPOGRAPHIC WORK.

BY MARK B. KERR.

In addition to the ascent of Mount St. Elias, it was part of the original plan of the expedition to make an accurate topographic map of the region explored. It was not, however, for this purpose proposed to divide the party or to deviate much from the most direct route to Mount St. Elias from Yakutat bay. Triangulation of fair precision was provided for. Details were to be filled in by approximate methods.

Field-work began June 20 by the careful measurement of a base-line, 3,850 feet in length, near the point of landing, on the northern shore of Yakutat bay. Expansion was readily carried to the foot-hills, and several horizontal angles were taken to an astronomical station of the United States Coast and Geodetic Survey at Port Mulgrave. In the region of these initial triangles, work was done from a central camp; and topographic details were fixed with considerable precision by intersection and vertical angles.

After the departure of the expedition from the Base Line camp, an accident to the transit made resort to an inferior instrument necessary, and, furthermore, as the region traversed proved to be ill-adapted to, and the line of travel too direct for, the proper development of a narrow belt of triangles, the anticipation of a degree of precision in the triangulation which would give high value to the determinations of position and altitude of the several peaks was not realized; but topographic map work, showing the general features, altitudes and location of the mountain ranges, valleys and glaciers, was extended over about 600 square miles.

Within the approximate geometric control, stations were interpolated by the three-point method, and minor locations were multiplied by intersection and connected by sketch. The best meander possible under the circumstances was carried forward on the line of travel by compass directions and estimates of distance from time intervals. The work ceased August 22 with the abandonment of the instruments in a snow-storm of four days' duration on the eastern slope of Mount St. Elias.

The accompanying map (a reduction of which forms plate 8, page 75) shows the ice-streams and peculiar mountain topography of a region heretofore unvisited, and constitutes a considerable addition to the geography of Alaska.

Appendix C.

REPORT ON AURIFEROUS SANDS FROM YAKUTAT BAY.

BY J. STANLEY-BROWN.

Among the specimens obtained by Mr. I. C. Russell during the course of his explorations on and about Mount St. Elias is a bottle of sand procured from the beach on the extreme southern end of Khantaak island, Yakutat bay, and characteristic of the shore material over a large area. This sand was turned over to me for examination, and additional interest was given to its study by the fact that it is from a comparatively uninvestigated region and possesses, perhaps, economic value; for the sample is gold-bearing, and it is said that a "color" can readily be obtained by "panning" at many points on the bay shore.

Macroscopically, the sand has the appearance of ordinary finely comminuted beach material; but it differs in the uniformity of the size of its particles from beach sand from Fort Monroe and Sullivan island, South Carolina, with which it was compared. Its mineralogic constituents greatly surpass in variety those of the sands referred to, but are markedly similar to those of gold-bearing sand from New Zealand. At least twelve minerals are present, with an unusual predominance of one, as will be noted later. Through the mixture of white, green, and black grains, a dull greenish-black color is given to the mass. The roundness of fragments is such as usually results from water action, but it is less than that which results from transportation by wind.

When put into a heavy liquid (Thoulet solution of a density of 3.4) in order to determine the specific gravity of the constituents, it was found that the sand is made up largely of the heavier materials, for the amount that floated was trifling compared with that which quickly sank. Even the abundant quartz was largely carried down by the weightier ingredients bound up within it, and only a few water-clear fragments were left behind. This would seem to suggest that the lighter minerals are lacking in the neighboring rocks, or else have been carried to greater distances by the sorting power of the water.

Among the minerals recognized, gold is the most important, though relatively not abundant. It occurs in flakes or flattened grains from a quarter to a half of a millimeter in size. The particles are sufficiently numerous to be readily selected from their associates by the aid of "panning" and a hand lens of good magnifying power, and if distributed throughout the beach as plentifully as in the sample would, under favorable conditions, pay for working. The flakes in their rounded character show the effect of the agency which separated them from their matrix; a separation so complete that no rock is found adhering to the grains.

(196)

Magnetite is present in great abundance and in a finely divided state, the largest grains not exceeding a millimeter in length. It forms by weight alone 15 or 20 per cent. of the entire mass, and when the latter is sifted through a sieve of a hundred meshes to the inch it constitutes 44 per cent. of this fine material. Crystallographic faces are rare, and though often marred, still octahedrons (111, 1) of considerable perfection are found.

Garnet occurs in such profusion that a pink tint is given to a mass of selected grains of uniform size, and its predominance may be considered the chief physical characteristic of the sand.

Two species were noted: one is a brilliant wine-red variety, which, though not nearly so numerous as its duller relative, occurs more frequently in crystals—the trapezohedral faces (211, 2-2) predominating. The other garnet is readily distinguished by its lighter amethystine tint and its greater abundance. Crystallographic faces are somewhat rare and invariably dodecahedral (110, i). In the absence of chemical analyses, any statements as to the exact species to which these garnets should be referred would be largely conjectural. Attention is quickly drawn to the perfection of these minute garnets in their crystallographic faces and outlines, and to their association with rounded fragments of their own kind as well as of other minerals. Have these crystals survived by reason of their hardness or by favoring conditions, or does their preservation suggest the impotency of wave-action in the destruction of minute bodies?

Among the black, heavy grains occur individuals which, except in shape and non-magnetic character, resemble magnetite. On crushing between glass slides, thin slivers are obtained which in transmitted light are green, and which, from their cleavage, pleochroism, high index of refraction, small extinction angle, and insolubility in acid, are readily recognized as hornblende.

Two groups of grains were noted which are distinguishable by slight variation in color. Both are clear-yellowish green, but one is somewhat darker than the other. The optical properties of both indicate pyroxene and possibly olivine. Fortunately a fragment was obtained in the ortho-diagonal zone nearly normal to an optic axis which gave an axial figure of sufficient definiteness to indicate its optically positive character. A number of grains were selected from minerals of both colors and subjected to prolonged heating in hydrochloric acid without decomposition, indicating that both minerals are pyroxene.

A few zircons, a fraction of a millimeter in size but perfect in form, were found associated with others rounded on their solid angles and edges. The crystals are of the common short form and bear the usual faces in a greater or less degree of development. Pyramids of the first and second order alternate in magnitude; pinacoid encroaches upon prism, and *vice versa*.

Quartz constitutes by far the largest proportion of the minerals, both in bulk and in weight. It is always fragmental; sometimes water-clear, but chiefly occurs in opaque grains of different colors. It is seldom free from material of a higher specific gravity, and is often so tinted as to be almost indistinguishable from magnetite, but readily bleaches in acid.

Feldspar is sparingly present, and includes both monoclinic and triclinic forms, whose crystallographic boundaries are invariably lacking.

Treatment of the sand with dilute acid produces effervescence, which is not due to incrustations of sodium carbonate. By persistent search among particles separated in a heavy solution, a few grains were discovered which, from their complete solubility with effervescence in very dilute acid, as well as their optical properties, left no doubt as to their being calcite.

The mica group has only one representative, biotite, and this occurs most sparingly. Though much of the sand was examined, but few fragments were found. Its foliated character renders it easily transported by water and explains its absence from among the heavy minerals.

Shaly, slaty and schistose material forms the major part of the coarser grains. Thin sections from the largest pieces plainly indicated hornblende schist.

A region of glaciers would seem to be favorable not only to the collection of meteoric material, but also to the destruction of the country rocks, the setting free of their mineralogic constituents in a comparatively fresh state, and their transportation to the sea. It was hoped that this sand would yield some of the rarer varieties of minerals, but tests for native iron, platinum, chromite, gneiss, and the titaniferous minerals proved ineffectual. Titanium is present, but in such small quantities that it could only be detected by means of hydrogen peroxide. The use of acid supersulphate and the borotungstate of calcium test of Lasaulx failed to reveal the presence of native iron.

It will be seen from the foregoing enumeration that the sand is made up of grains of gold, magnetite, garnet, hornblende, pyroxene, zircon, quartz, feldspar, calcite and mica, associated with fragments of a shaly, slaty and schistose character. While the information at hand is hardly sufficient to warrant much speculation concerning the rock masses of the interior, still there is no doubt that the sand is derived from the destruction of metamorphic rocks.

APPENDIX D.

REPORT ON FOSSIL PLANTS.

BY LESTER F. WARD.

DEPARTMENT OF THE INTERIOR,
UNITED STATES GEOLOGICAL SURVEY,
Washington, D. C., March 12, 1891.

Mr. I. C. RUSSELL,
United States Geological Survey.

MY DEAR SIR: The following report upon the small collection of fossil plants made by you at Pinnacle pass, near Mount St. Elias, Alaska, and sent to this division for identification has been prepared by Professor F. H. Knowlton, who gave the collection a careful study during my absence in Florida. Previous to going away I had somewhat hastily examined the specimens and seen that they consisted chiefly of the genus *Salix*, some of them reminding me strongly of living species. I have no doubt that Professor Knowlton's more thorough comparisons can be relied upon with as much confidence as the nature of the collection will permit, and I also agree with his conclusions.

" The collection consists of seven small hand specimens, upon which are impressed no less than seventeen more or less completely preserved dicotyledonous leaves.

" These specimens at first sight seem to represent six or eight species, but after a careful study I think I am safe in reducing the number to four, as several of the impressions have been nearly obliterated by prolonged exposure and cannot be studied with much satisfaction.

" The four determinable species belong, without much doubt, to the genus *Salix*. Number 1, of which there is but a single specimen, I have identified with *Salix californica*, Lesquereux, from the auriferous gravel deposits of the Sierra Nevada in California.[*] The finer nervation of the specimens from the auriferous gravels is not clearly shown in Lesquereux's figures, nor is it well preserved in the Mount St. Elias specimens; but the size, outline, and primary nervation are identical.

" Number 2, of which there are six or eight specimens, may be compared with *Salix cucana*, Heer,[†] a species that was first described from Greenland and was later detected by Lesquereux in a collection from Cooks inlet, Alaska.[‡] The Mount St. Elias specimens are not very much like the original figures of Heer, but are very similar, in outline at least, to this species as figured by Lesquereux.[§] They are also very similar to

[*] Mem. Mus. Comp. Zool., vol. VI, no. 2, 1878, p. 10, pl. i, figs. 18-21.
[†] Flor. foss. Arct., vol. I, 1868, p. 102, pl. iv, figs. 11-13; pl. xlvii, fig. 11.
[‡] Proc. Nat. Mus., vol. V, 1882, p. 447.
[§] loc. cit., pl. viii, fig. 6.

some forms of the living *S. rostrata*, Richardson, with entire leaves. It is clearly a willow, but closer identification must remain for more complete material.

"Number 3, represented by four or five specimens, is broadly elliptical in outline, and is also clearly a *Salix*. It is unlike any fossil form with which I am familiar, but is very similar to the living *S. nigricans*, For., var. *rotundifolia*, and to certain forms of *S. silesiaca*, Willd. The nervation is very distinctly preserved, and has all the characters of a willow leaf.

"Number 4, represented by three or four very fine specimens, is a very large leaf, measuring 13 cm. in length and 3½ cm. in width at the broadest point. It may be compared with *Salix macrophylla*, Heer,* but it cannot be this species. It is also like some of the living forms of *S. nigra*, Marsh., from which it differs in having perfectly entire margins.

"While it is manifestly impossible, on the basis of the above identifications, to speak with confidence as to the age or formation containing these leaves, it can hardly be older than the Miocene, and from its strong resemblance to the present existing flora of Alaska it is likely to be much younger." [F. H. Knowlton.]

Very sincerely yours,   LESTER F. WARD.

* Tert. Fl. Helv., vol. II, 1856, p. 29, pl. lxvii, fig. 4.

www.ingramcontent.com/pod-product-compliance
Lightning Source LLC
Chambersburg PA
CBHW030606040726
47497CB00008B/2864